Praise for Dragon's Truth

"Love, adventure, sacrifice, honor, wisdom, tragedy, and triumph – this epic tale has it all. This powerful, lyrical, and original novel will take every reader on a walk down the prismed path created by Leanne M. Pankuch. I loved this unforgettable journey! – T. A. Barron, author of *The Merlin Saga*

Adventure and mystery intertwine in this brilliant debut fantasy." - Megg Jensen, USA Today bestselling author of the Dragonlands series

Leanne Pankuch's beguiling fantasy novel draws from the wells of Welsh and Anglo-Saxon mythology but stays grounded in the rivalries, ambitions and affections of its original characters. Rhyan, a turbulent younger sibling, is refreshingly self-aware as she joins forces with an apprentice gardener, a Faerie lord, and the son of her greatest enemy on the perilous quest to save her sister. – Alisa Kwitney, author of *Corpse and Crown*

"...Dragon's Truth kept me turning pages. The emotional impact came from several inspiring, memorable characters. The protagonist is a strong female who well understands the importance of collaborating and communicating in a polite way, a lesson particularly timely in today's society." – Gayl Smith, MLS, retired K-12 Teacher/Librarian

"In *Dragon's Truth*, Leanne Pankuch brings to life a rich tapestry of fantastical events with winning characters at the center who compel us to follow their journey as if it were our own. And like

the most enduring journey sagas of myth and legend, from the 16th century story, Monkey King, Journey to the West, to the Arthurian cycle, to Tolkien's *The Hobbit* and Marissa Meyer's contemporary *Lunar Chronicles*, this story not only proves magical, lush, and suspenseful at all the twists and turns along the way, but also sheds light on the big questions of human identity— how we learn about ourselves, how we experience family and friendship, what it takes to overcome disappointment and handle success, and what is worth fighting for, not just for ourselves, but on behalf of those who depend on us. With a deft pallet of storytelling elements — vividly defined settings, unexpected plot developments, and motifs that invite new and evolving perspectives on her female heroine and companions, Pankuch enlists her most satisfying ingredient—affection for and commitment to her universe of protagonists: the deserving, the imperfect, the deeply flawed, the larger than life, whether they be Faerie, horse, or human, whether their powers elevate or diminish. The result is an utterly engrossing saga that will keep you engaged well beyond these pages—asking for more."
– Francine G Navakas, PhD, Svend and Elizabeth Bramsen Professor Emerita in the Humanities, North Central College

DRAGON'S TRUTH

LEANNE M. PANKUCH

Formatted by Woven Red Autthor Servicess, www.WovenRed.ca

Print book ISBN: 978-1-7327112-2-8

Library of Congress Cataloging-in-Publication Data
Pankuch, Leanne, author
Dragon's Truth
Ladson, South Carolina: Vinspire Publishing [2019]
LCCN: 2019932777 (print)|ISBN 978-1-7327112-3-5 (pb)|
BISAC: YOUNG ADULT/FANTASY

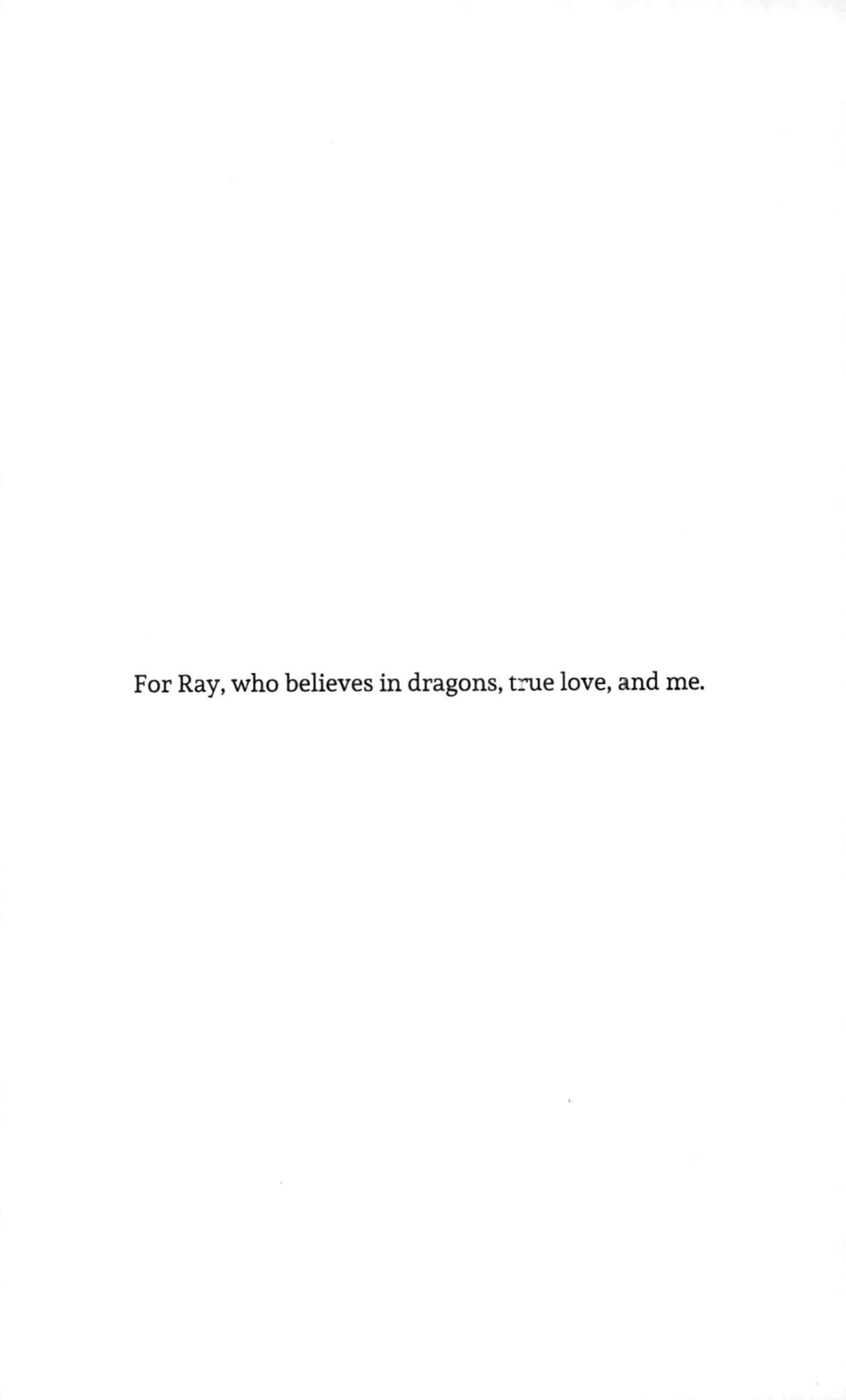

For Ray, who believes in dragons, true love, and me.

Contents

Characters

Of Kember and Rivertown

Rhyannon Kember – youngest niece of Lord Angus Kember

Elspeth Kember – oldest niece of Lord Angus Kember

Lord Angus Kember – feudal lord of Caer Kember and lands south of the Whyte Clyffs

Lady Rosamund Kember – aunt of Rhyan and Elspeth

Lord Dylan Kember – deceased brother of Lord Angus, father of Rhyan and Elspeth

Lady Branwen Kember – deceased mother of Rhyan and Elspeth

Nanny Bess – nurse and governess to Rhyan and Elspeth

Old Llud – longtime gardener at Caer Kember

Collen William's Son – grandson of Old Llud

Of Windover

Prince Evnis Plendraig – feudal lord of Windover and lands north of the Whyte Clyffs

Hale Plendraig – heir to Prince Evnis

Lady Nonnell Plendraig – wife of Prince Evnis

Of Eadarowan

Sianne, the Eldest – leader and wise woman of the Fairie

Ailem Suir, First Son of Faerie – Sianne's grandson

Feärn, Eldest of Alder – a Fairie lord

Linné, Second Daughter of Sellé – Sianne's granddaughter

Tura, First Daughter of Alder – a Fairie warrior

Fiona Wyddandaughter – a Fairie without a family

Darkmane – Windhoove assigned to Tura of Alder

Duskmane – Windhoove assigned to Ailem Suir
Fierceheart – Windhoove assigned to Man Lyr
Firefoot – Windhoove assigned to Hale Plendraig
Starlight – Windhoove assigned to Rhyan Kember
Surefoot – Windhoove assigned to Collen William's son
The Kirrin – mythical guardian of the forest lands and the Faerie people

Of Dalria
Morgan macNeill – Steward of Dalria
Garth macNeill – uncle of Morgan macNeill
Dowager Lady macNeill – grandmother of Morgan macNeill
Dougal Fraser – head of clan Fraser
Taran macNeill – a former steward of Dalria
Bridelyn – ancient princess and mage-ruler of Dalria

Of the Kanesga Plainsland
Kel Dana – warrior of the Kanesga and sister of Kai Mostfa
Kai Mostfa – chieftain of the Kanesga

Wanderers and Wizards
Keven Tralleigh – son of the Trallendon royal family
Man Lyr – tutor and mentor of Rhyan Kember
Druin Canwyr – dark wizard and dragon-lord
Dark Knight of Cumbria – legendary sell-sword who served an ancient king of Kember
Kara Falcon – sentient bird from across the Diamond Sea

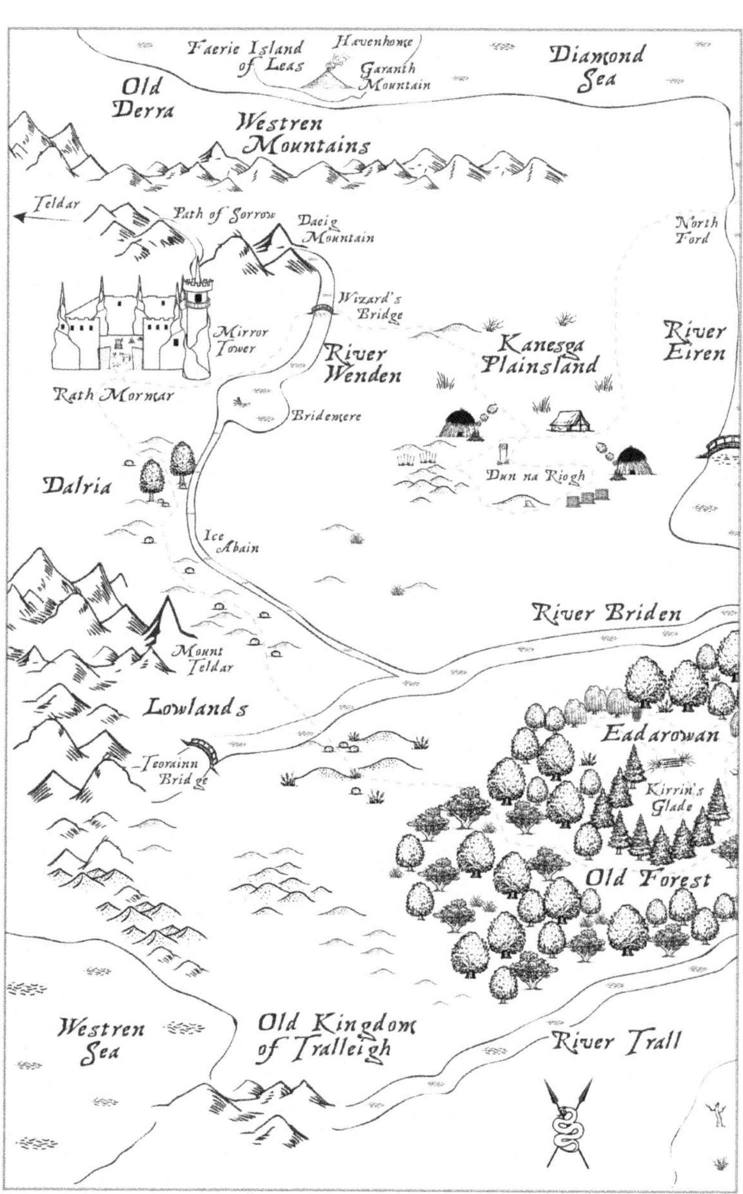

Old Derra
Faerie Island of Leas
Havenhome
Garanth Mountain
Diamond Sea
Westren Mountains
Teldar
Path of Sorrow
Daeig Mountain
North Ford
Wizard's Bridge
Mirror Tower
River Wenden
Kanesga Plainsland
River Eiren
Rath Mormar
Bridemere
Dalria
Dun na Riogh
Ice Abain
River Briden
Mount Teldar
Lowlands
Eadarowan
Kirrin's Glade
Teorainn Bridge
Old Forest
Westren Sea
Old Kingdom of Tralleigh
River Trall

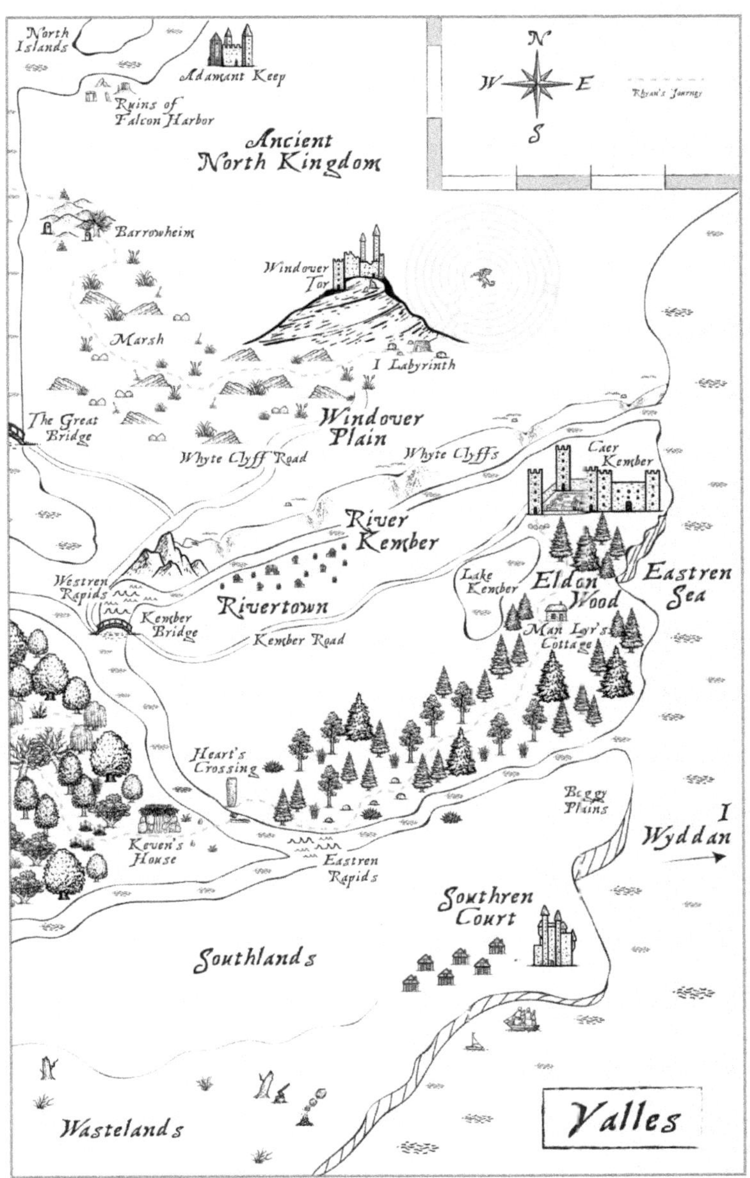
North Islands
Adamant Keep
Ruins of Falcon Harbor
Ancient North Kingdom
N
W
E
S
Rhyan's Journey
Barrowheim
Windover Tor
Marsh
I Labyrinth
The Great Bridge
Windover Plain
Whyte Clyff Road
Whyte Clyffs
Caer Kember
River Kember
Lake Kember
Eldan Wood
Eastren Sea
Westren Rapids
Rivertown
Kember Bridge
Kember Road
Man Loy's Cottage
Heart's Crossing
Beggy Plains
Keven's House
Wyddan
Eastren Rapids
Southren Court
Southlands
Wastelands
Valles

ONE

A Storm

Rhyan lay motionless at the base of the ancient pine. Heavy, sagging branches hid her from view. She closed her eyes and breathed in the rich, tangy smell of the drying needles and sticky sap.

If I were a wizard, I would take a deer's shape, and this is where I would sleep.

The tree's fragrant scent soothed her. As her body relaxed, dream-images filled her restless mind.

Silent he walks in the shadows of the forest.

A dark-armored hunter with black bow in hand.

He nocks a red-fletched arrow and points it toward the heart of the sleeping deer.

CRACK! Thunder shook the air.

Rhyan's eyes flew open and the troubling dream fled. She poked her head out of the pine boughs and glanced up. A break in the green ceiling of Eldon Wood revealed boiling black clouds.

We're going to get wet.

"Rhyan!" Elspeth called from the other side of the tree. "I give up. The win is yours. Hurry out before we're caught in the rain."

Rhyan pulled her head back under the branches and crawled around to where Elspeth stood.

Oh, how sweet this would be! It almost wasn't fair.

"Ha!" Rhyan reached out from her hiding place to grab her sister's ankle.

"Aieee!" Elspeth screeched. "You scared the life out of me!"

Rhyan climbed from her hiding place, laughing. "Lucky for you that the weather has turned, dear sister," she teased. "Otherwise you'd have searched until sunset."

"It's lucky for *you* that I still play this childish game, *little* sister." Elspeth threw her an annoyed glance. "You carry on as if you were years younger than me instead of just minutes. Covered in dirt and leaves—just look at those skirts! You're like a woodland creature or a sly and shabby fairie!"

Rhyan's hand shot out to cover her sister's mouth. "Don't insult them here, El," she whispered.

Elspeth pulled away and tossed bright golden curls. "Don't tell me you still believe that nonsense? We're almost fourteen turnings now! You should start acting like a proper lady and forget—"

"I don't want to be a proper lady! We may be twins but I'm *not* like you! Man Lyr says—"

"Don't even speak his name!" Elspeth interrupted. "Nanny says our uncle is wrong to allow that man to teach you. He is a forest hermit and a heathen."

Rhyan clenched her fists. "You lecture me for believing in the Faerie when *you* listen to the rambling fears of an old woman? Aunt Rose and Uncle Angus chose Man Lyr to be my tutor! He could teach you, too—if you ever wanted to learn more than dance steps and how to tie a perfect bow."

Lightning flashed as thunder cracked and boomed. Elspeth squealed, glancing up at the menacing clouds. The sky opened and rain poured down.

Without another word, Rhyan grabbed her sister's hand and the two girls ran homeward.

The driving rain fell like liquid arrows, piercing Eldon Wood's dense, leafy canopy. Rhyan's soaked skirts clung to her legs. She struggled to lead her sister through the forest.

Elspeth tripped and fell into a large, muddy puddle, pulling Rhyan down as well. "Just look at me!" She struggled to her feet. "My gown is utterly ruined!"

Rolling her eyes, Rhyan stood and wiped mud from her hands on to her already-stained skirt.

A sudden chill of unease brushed across her spine like the fingers of a spectral hand. Without warning, fierce wind gusts bent and twisted the thick, sturdy limbs of the trees that surrounded them.

Rhyan shouted over the crash and thrash of branches. "We need to find shelter—this storm feels wrong!" Taking her sister's hand once more, she turned back and found the stone waypost marking the path to Man Lyr's cottage.

They rushed up the pebbled walk, and Rhyan pounded her fist against the familiar *M* rune carved into the heavy oak door.

Please let him be home!

The door swung open, and she and Elspeth slipped inside, both gasping for breath. Elspeth sobbed.

"We're safe now, El." Rhyan slid an arm around her sister.

Her friend and tutor, the forest sage Man Lyr, closed the door against the raging weather. "Be still," the old man whispered. He pointed toward the fireplace.

Rhyan obeyed. She peered into the semi-darkened room. Was someone there? When her eyes adjusted to the firelight, she gasped. A great snowy falcon perched on the mantle over the hearth. The bird's long talons dug into the wood.

Oh, how beautiful!

Elspeth sneezed.

The ice-blue eyes of the falcon found them. White wings began to spread.

Rhyan raised her hands to protect her sister.

Man Lyr rushed forward and slipped a cloth over the bird's head. The falcon settled back onto the mantle as the old man stroked its breast, murmuring soft, soothing sounds. The falcon chirped and cawed. Man Lyr's voice clicked and whirred in answer.

Beautiful and dangerous.

"Where did it come from?" Rhyan finally dared to speak.

"She is Kara Falcon." Man Lyr uncovered the head of the quieted bird. "Her home is to the north—across the Diamond Sea. She reached Eldon Wood just as the storm erupted, and a strong gust of wind flung her against something hard—a tree perhaps, she can't remember. I found her knocked senseless on my doorstep minutes before you arrived."

Kara Falcon blinked and cocked her head to the side. Her sharp blue gaze studied Rhyan.

"She told you this? You spoke to her?" Rhyan caught her breath. *Oh…to possess such a talent!* "I wish that I might speak to birds, sir."

Man Lyr fixed deep gray eyes on her. "And what would you do with such a great power, Little Dragon? What if I told you that speaking to birds was the least of your abilities and that enchantment flows swift and strong in your blood?"

In a flash, Rhyan saw herself as a great sorceress. Seated on a silver throne in a clear glass castle with an infant dragon asleep at her feet, she, Rhyannon the Great, would dispense wisdom to all who sought her aid.

"Nonsense! Little Dragon, *indeed.*" Elspeth sneezed again, and then rubbed her nose with a wet handkerchief.

"Forgive me, Lady Elspeth." Man Lyr bowed. "Come close to the fire—both of you. Spiced cider brews even now. I will fetch towels and water, so you may wash the mud from your hands."

Lady Elspeth, indeed. Rhyan cast a wry look at her old friend. She and her sister sat on wooden chairs flanking the small hearth table.

Rhyan knew Man Lyr saw the yearning spirit that struggled inside her. Her heart swelled every time he called her *Little Dragon*. During her lessons, he'd often hinted that her future held far greater things than the boring existence awaiting ordinary, prim and proper *Lady* Elspeth.

Man Lyr took the falcon from the room. He returned with a bowl of warm rosewater and a stack of clean cloths. "I'll be but a few more minutes attending to Kara Falcon. Please—rest and refresh." He bowed again before leaving them.

Elspeth picked up a cloth and dipped one corner into the bowl. With dainty precision, she dabbed at the thick globs of dried mud spattered across her pale cheeks.

"It won't come off like that." Rhyan picked up her own towel and soaked it in the water. "You're simply smearing it around." She gripped Elspeth's chin and scrubbed at the dirt.

"Oww! You'll mark my face!" Elspeth tried to pull away.

But Rhyan held tight. "I'm not hurting you."

"Just because *you* don't care a whit about your appearance! Nanny Bess says—"

"Stones and bones! *Nanny* this and *Nanny* that! Can't you ever think for yourself? What will you do when Nanny isn't taking care of you anymore?"

Elspeth squirmed out of Rhyan's grip. "You're just jealous because your skin is so sallow-brown and covered with sunspots!"

"At least I'm not as pale as a turnip," Rhyan shot back.

The old man returned. He swung a steaming pot out of the hearth and filled mugs with the hot, fragrant drink.

The cider warmed Rhyan, but her mud-spattered clothes remained damp a half an hour later when the storm passed Eldon Wood and took its fury into the Southlands. She pointed out that Elspeth's skirt wasn't yet dry either, and suggested they stay a little longer.

"Nanny Bess will be angry if we're tardy to the dinner table again." Elspeth lifted her chin with a familiar stubbornness.

Rhyan bit her lip.

What harm would a few more minutes do?

Man Lyr, his arm wrapped with a thick, protective towel, brought the white falcon back into the room. He carried on a gentle conversation in Kara's language and the bird's apprehension melted away like ice exposed to the warm sun.

How is it that I know what this bird is feeling?

Rhyan gasped as Kara's piercing blue eyes turned her way.

'Because you are a dragon-child.'

The words echoed in Rhyan's mind. Had Kara spoken to her?

"Man Lyr! I think the falcon—"

"Another day, my young friend," Man Lyr opened the front door. "Ah, look, the Goddess sends a rainbow—there in the westren sky. We can be assured the storm is over, then."

"But sir, I want—"

"No more delays, Lady Rhyannon. Your sister is right, you should return to the castle. Doubtless your aunt and uncle will worry over your absence.'

Man Lyr took Elspeth's hand as she came to the door. "Someday I will meet your revered Nanny and convince her that I am not what she fears."

Elspeth bobbed a quick curtsey and hurried outside.

Rhyan reluctantly followed. "Perhaps we should stay just a little longer? I have so many questions. I think—"

"We will speak of this later." Man Lyr interrupted again. He glanced at Elspeth, then bent his head and spoke in a whisper for Rhyan's ears alone. "You must get quickly home, Little Dragon. Some ill was in the wind of that storm. You felt it and Kara Falcon had a taste of it, as well. Remember our lesson on the ancient calendar? Today is the old feast of *Gwyl Ifan*—Midsummer—a day when the magic of the land is powerful and the veil between worlds is thin. Somehow, I failed to read the signs and recognize the danger. Watch out for Elspeth...she does not see with your eyes."

"What is it, sir?" Rhyan shivered again with the same fey

chill that touched her during the storm.

"Evil." The old man's whispered answer hung in the air like the final toll of a ghostly bell.

The cold in Rhyan's bones turned to ice.

TWO

Visitors

"Hurry, El! Let's sneak in the kitchen door." Rhyan grabbed her sister's hand and led her through the West Gate and up the worn stone stairs of the servants' entrance.

"Are these two young *ladies* I see before me?" Nanny Bess caught them just outside the door. She thumped her hands on her round hips. "I mistook you for half-drowned sheep!"

Rhyan rolled her eyes.

"We're sorry, Nanny." Elspeth hung her head.

"Oh, I don't doubt that you are now that I've caught you. Where have you been?"

"We were walking in the forest when the storm hit." Elspeth's voice trembled.

Nanny reached out to finger the fabric of Elspeth's skirt. She raised an eyebrow. "Your gown is nearly dry."

"Man Lyr gave us shelter." Rhyan cringed as a horrified expression appeared on Nanny's face.

"What? That wicked hermit?"

"He spoke to a falcon, Nanny," Rhyan burst out. "It was as

white as snow, with eyes like the sky! Man Lyr said that—"

"Don't say another word!" The old woman covered her ears. "Heathen sorcery it is! Just wait until Lord Angus hears of this. Talking to wild birds...he must forbid this *tutoring* now."

"He was quite polite and kind to us, Nanny." Elspeth surprised Rhyan with her defense of Man Lyr. "Very respectful."

Nanny Bess shook her head. "I expect this behavior from Rhyan, but you, Elspeth? If you hadn't been playing in the forest like peasant children, you wouldn't have had to take shelter with that...that...*man*! It grieves my heart. Will you ever begin to act like noble-born ladies?" She sniffled, rubbing her large nose with the over-embroidered handkerchief she always carried.

Rhyan sighed. *I'll never be what Nanny wants. Never.*

"We'll talk about punishment later." Nanny pulled herself up straight. "Head up to your room and get presentable, ladies. Thank goodness I had the maids ready your baths. I've scented yours with rosewater, just as you like, Elspeth. Do put on something suitable, Rhyan. That lovely russet silk will be fine."

I won't be able to breathe—never mind eat!

"But Nanny—"

"Hush now, not another word! We've important visitors— the Prince of Windover is Lord Angus's guest this evening."

A strange tension rang in Nanny's voice when she mentioned the Prince of Windover. It jarred in Rhyan's ears like a note out of tune.

"Why is the prince coming to dinner tonight, Nanny?" Rhyan kept a sharp eye on the old woman's expression. "He has never visited Caer Kember before, has he?"

Nanny brushed distractedly at her own skirt and did not meet Rhyan's eyes. "I'm sure I don't pretend to know the business of the noble-born."

She's hiding something.

"Mind what I've told you, Elspeth." Nanny lifted a gnarled finger. "We eat at six bells."

"Yes, ma'am." Elspeth pulled Rhyan through the hall door.

When they reached the wide staircase that led to the castle's private chambers, Rhyan stopped and faced her sister. "Something about this feels strange."

"Don't make a fuss, Rhyan. I want to wear my blue gown with the lace sleeves. You know it takes forever to do up the ties, not to mention the time I need to dry my hair after a bath. And I need to check the mark you made on my face!"

"It's all but faded, silly." Rhyan put a gentle hand to her sister's rosy cheek. "I just want to know why the prince is coming to see Uncle."

Elspeth shrugged. "What does it matter? Perhaps it's about the Southren Court Council or those renegade tribesmen in westren Trall. Uncle's always discussing politics with someone."

"Didn't you notice how Nanny didn't want to talk about it? That alone is strange—we know how she loves to gossip. And besides that, it's odd that the prince has never come here before, don't you think? Windover is so close and Uncle Angus and Aunt Rose have visited there many times."

"Perhaps the prince doesn't like children." Elspeth started up the stairs. "And you are *such* a child, Rhyan—making a mystery out of nothing, like a little goose-girl! Man Lyr is at fault for these wild imaginings! All his magic-talk has you overly excited. Nanny told us to get dressed and that's what we're going to do."

"You go ahead. I'll be up shortly." Rhyan turned and ran down the hall.

"Be quick or I'll send the maid for you," Elspeth called after her.

Skirting busy servants lighting candles and torches along the main hall, Rhyan hurried to the side door that led to the castle gardens. Old Llud would know all there was to tell about the Prince of Windover. After all, he'd been the chief gardener at Caer Kember since before Uncle Angus's birth.

She pushed open the door and walked outside. To the left, tall, arched shrubs marked the entrance to the hedge maze.

Rhyan turned right, toward the open gate of the castle garden. Peach-pink foxglove, sky blue phlox, and bright yellow hollyhocks bloomed against the dark green ivy-covered walls. The garden's heavy perfume, an invisible kaleidoscope of candied scent, tickled Rhyan's nose as she rushed along the pathway of flat, white stone that wound around wooden benches and weeping tree roses. At the center of the grounds stood a statue of a young girl with a bouquet of wildflowers in her white marble hands. A tiny bird with red-tipped wings rested on the statue's shoulder.

Rhyan stopped mid-stride to watch the small creature.

Where have you come from, little red-wing? What skies have you traveled?

The bird cocked its brown head and fixed a shining black-bead eye on her, but it made no reply.

Maybe I was wrong.

Off in one corner, Old Llud's white head bobbed up and down amid a patch of purple flowers. The gardener prided himself on Caer Kember's lavender. Rhyan stepped over and around the fragrant plants as she made her way through and knelt beside her old friend.

"How did you get by your Nanny looking such a mess, lady?" The old man glanced up from his weeding with a sparkle in his deep brown eyes.

"I didn't. I should be making myself more presentable at this very moment. Elspeth and I were out in the storm. The wind nearly blew us away!"

"Aye, lady. That were no natural storm—more like a battle! Mother Goddess tryin' to fight off somethin'. I was inspectin' the herb room stores for Lady Rose and didn't even know about the thunder 'n rain until young Collen, son of my own William, came to check on me after it blew by. He'd seen fallen trees and flattened crops in the fields near town and was worried about his old Grandad."

"I'm glad you were indoors, Llud. The storm left terrible

scars on the forest. 'Twas indeed like a battleground. Was the garden damaged?"

"No, thank the Crown and Ring, it's sheltered some by the castle walls. Is that why you are here when you should be dressing for dinner, young lady? To check on your posies? And your favorite old gardener?"

Rhyan smiled. "No. Although I'm glad all is well, I came to ask you something about tonight's visit from the Prince of Windover."

"What of him?" Llud turned back to his work and thrust his trowel into the ground.

I was right. There is *a secret here.*

"Why won't anyone talk about him?" she asked. "Just who *is* the Prince of Windover?"

As if her question held some magic power, a strange silence fell upon the garden. Even the birds stopped singing to listen for Old Llud's answer. The gardener bent his head. For a long minute he breathed in and out, in and out.

"So help me, I cannot keep the truth from ye any longer, my sweet, strong girl." When at last he spoke, sadness and resignation weighted his kind voice. "We of the household have been forbidden to speak of it to you or your sister—though tonight's visit will change that, for sure and certain."

Llud held up a blue harebell that he had dug from the flower bed, its delicate stem and smooth, hooded shape a showy contrast against the compact spikes of sturdy lavender.

"Your mother loved this garden. Like a flower herself she was—willowy and golden-bright. Always dressed in her favorite rose-red color. Beautiful on the inside, too—a true daughter of the Goddess." Llud set the harebell in a clay pot, pulled a tattered handkerchief from his pocket, and rubbed his eyes. "But for all her gentle beauty and loving feelings toward him, her own brother rejected her."

Rhyan gasped. "A brother?"

Llud nodded. "A twin brother. But although they shared a

birthin' day, your mother Branwen was firstborn. As her birth-right, she received an ancient gift, while her womb-mate—male and his father's heir—was left empty-handed.

"As the years passed, her brother's heart grew gray and twisted like a dead tree. All the darkest parts of humankind seemed to come together in him—so hurtful and hateful he became! He blamed Branwen, innocent though she was. And he seemed to feel nothing when she and her young husband were killed in an accident. Worst of all, Prince Evnis refused to take you and Elspeth into his care."

Rhyan's mouth dropped open.

"Aye, my dear." Old Llud dipped his chin in a single, heavy nod. "Prince Evnis of Windover is your uncle."

THREE

Uncle Evnis

Rhyan stood near the open shutters of her bedroom window. She stared out into the main courtyard of the castle, trying to keep still as Elspeth fussed with the intricate back lacings of her gown.

As always, the square was nearly empty this close to dinner. Only the Watchguard stood at their posts, waiting for the evening bell and the closing of the gate.

In a last display of brilliance, sunset painted the distant sky in oranges, bronzes, and purples. Rhyan's gaze lifted past the walls of Caer Kember to the northwestren horizon. Was that the outline of Windover Tor against the rich colors? The Prince of Windover's castle fortress crowned the flat-topped mountain and shared its name.

Rhyan's lips parted. She wanted to draw Elspeth's attention to the beautiful sky, but the burnt rainbow disappeared as quickly as it had flared. Clouds gathered, and an early twilight fell. A strange swirling fog reached long, silent fingers over the outer castle walls and crept down into the yard. An unseasonable chill drifted in through the open window. Rhyan shivered with uneasy expectation. The Watchguard shifted and looked about. Were they nervous too? When the evening bell finally rang, the guards rushed to close the heavy doors of the main gate and lower the portcullis. Perhaps they joined her in breathing a sigh of relief.

A sharp rap on the chamber door startled her.

"Yes?"

One of the maids poked her head into the room. "Begging your ladies' pardon. Nanny Bess says dinner will be starting sharp on the hour." Without waiting for an answer, she nodded and closed the door.

"Hold still, Rhyan!" Elspeth tugged her back into position. "These laces are difficult to straighten when you keep jumping. What *is* the matter?"

"Oh, El…I can't tell you. Old Llud made me promise. But I'm sure we'll hear all about it at dinner."

Her sister yanked the laces tighter and Rhyan gasped. "I can't breathe!"

Sighing, Elspeth slackened her grip. "I didn't mean to hurt you. I'm just upset. You should have come up and dressed instead of running off! You know how I hate being late."

"I didn't run off, I just—"

"Never mind now. There, you're finished! And, honestly, you look quite pretty in that russet shade. Your eyes are positively golden, and your hair has a very fetching chestnut shine." Elspeth smiled. "Wait! One naughty strand has escaped the braid. There! Perfect. Your hair is so elegant when it's brushed and arranged properly."

"Thank you." Rhyan clenched her jaw. *Meaning, of course, that my hair is rarely brushed properly.*

"Aunt Rose's new maid taught me this style." Elspeth seemed oblivious of Rhyan's irritation. "It's called a battle braid–not too fussy, and easy to fix, so I thought you might like it. It really does suit your brown hair and lovely skin, you know."

"You needn't flatter me, El. You called my complexion sallow and sun-spotted while we were at Man Lyr's. I know I'll never be as beautiful as you."

Elspeth blushed. "Now *you're* flattering *me.*"

Rhyan did indeed find her sister even lovelier than usual in her new gown of rich cerulean blue. A net of snowy pearls held her burnished golden curls and her eyes sparkled. Elspeth was the sister who won the place of honor at feasts and celebrations. She was the Kember niece who pleased everyone.

How can twins be so different? Like day and night—and I am the night.

"If only you would spend a little time and effort to improve your manners and appearance." Elspeth adjusted the folds of her skirt. "You should give up playing in the woods and visiting forest hermits and old gardeners—"

"Then I'd be a dreadful snob, as you are!" Rhyan burst out.

Elspeth pressed her lips together. Raising her chin, she swung open the chamber door and swept out into the hallway.

Rhyan followed, seething. *Why does she make me so angry?*

Nanny waited at the entrance of the Great Hall. "Tsk, tsk," she clucked, looking the girls over. She tugged on one of Rhyan's laces and re-draped the folds of Elspeth's skirt. At last, she nodded her approval and sent them in.

Elspeth moved across the floor like a summer swan on Lake Kember. She stopped in front of the head table and performed a slow, controlled curtsey.

Too perfect. Nanny is probably watching at the entrance and crying for joy.

Rhyan took a deep breath and followed Elspeth across the floor. For a few moments, she thought she might not look ridiculous compared to her sister, but then, all was lost! As she did her best to imitate Elspeth's graceful curtsey, she wobbled, and put a hand on the rush-covered floor to keep her balance. Head down and teeth clenched—glad she couldn't see Nanny's face—

she stood, hurried to the chair next to her sister and sat down.

The dinner began with Lord Angus introducing his nieces to the Prince of Windover, his wife, Lady Nonnell, and their son Hale Plendraig.

Rhyan nodded, but in her embarrassment over the bobbled curtsey, she barely met their eyes. From there, the supper progressed in silence.

When curiosity at last overcame her discomfiture, Rhyan dared a look down the table at her newfound uncle and his family.

Lady Nonnell, a tiny wisp of a woman, sat to the right of Lord Angus. Hale of Windover, a thin, frowning, brown-haired boy of perhaps eleven or twelve years, sat next to his mother and tugged impatiently on her sleeve. Lady Nonnell and her son both wore cloth of silver trimmed in black.

Rhyan shifted her gaze to the place of honor. The Prince of Windover hadn't touched his plate. He sat next to Lady Rose, rigid, eyes fixed straight ahead. Pale skin pulled tight across the sharp bones of his face and threads of white in his brown-red hair made him appear older than Rhyan knew him to be. He wore a plain ink-black coat with a flaming dragon embroidered on the right breast. The dragon's diamond eyes flashed in the candlelight. Shivering, Rhyan looked down at her plate, her appetite gone.

No one ate much of anything. The servants carried platter after platter back to the kitchen barely touched. And no one spoke. As the meal continued, Rhyan's lack of appetite turned into a sick worry in the pit of her stomach.

Cook brought in the dessert course himself. His broad forehead bore a furrowed field of wrinkles. Lord Angus assured him that the meal was excellent, as always. Everyone had simply saved room for dessert. Cook waited until his master took a generous bite of the raspberry tart before he stomped off to the kitchen.

Lord Angus signaled the other servants and attendants in

the Great Hall. They exited in silence. Lady Rose paled and brought her handkerchief to her forehead.

What is happening?

Lord Angus rose and came to stand behind his two nieces.

"Rhyan, Elspeth, I have done what I thought best. If the truth you will hear this night...hurts you both, I beg forgiveness." He laid a hand on each of their shoulders.

The Prince of Windover stood. "I, Evnis Plendraig, am your uncle." His sharp, cold voice made no effort to cushion the news for his nieces.

Elspeth gasped.

"Your mother—my *sister*..."—the prince's lips twisted over the word as if tasting an unripe berry—"was born with the *Dragon's Gift,* our family legacy of power. As the male heir of our house, that power should rightfully belong to myself and my successor." He paused and cast a brief, icy glance at his wife and son. "I have spent long years searching for a means to undo this injustice, but the solution has been...elusive."

The Dragon's Gift, *our family legacy of power.* The wondrous words echoed in Rhyan's head. *I knew it! This is what I have waited for.*

Prince Evnis narrowed his gaze upon Elspeth. "So, my lady, as the eldest child of my sister and holder of the *Gift,* you will come to stay at Windover Tor. I will act as your guardian and provide for all your needs."

No! Rhyan bit her lip hard to keep from crying out loud. The metal-tang of blood touched her tongue. *No, Uncle, I am the one who holds this power. It* must *be me!*

"What...what about Rhyan?" Elspeth's wide, unbelieving eyes fixed on the prince.

Evnis's cold gaze flickered over Rhyan. "Your sister may visit you from time to time."

"My Lord Uncle," Elspeth faltered. "If I must leave my home...I wonder if Rhyan could not come with me...to stay? I would not—"

"Out of the question!" Prince Evnis interrupted.

"But, my lord—" Lady Nonnell spoke for the first time, her voice soft, hesitant.

"Silence! *I* have already decided this."

Lady Nonnell bowed her head.

Prince Evnis continued. "We will remove at once to Windover Tor."

"No!" Elspeth blurted out.

Rhyan stood. "Your pardon, Uncle, but my sister and I will not be parted! I will not allow you to take her." *And leave me behind!*

"You! *You* will not allow *me*?" The prince's dark eyes flashed. He leaned across the table as if he meant to grab Rhyan and shake her.

She stood her ground, raising her chin in response to her uncle's angry glare.

"Remember yourself, Evnis!" Lord Angus boomed. "Elspeth will be at Windover in time to perform the ritual. But I insist that Caer Kember remain her home."

"You must release the girl to me tonight, Angus! I need her now! It is imperative."

"You go too far! I will not be dictated to by a—"

"My Lords!" Lady Rose interrupted. "I insist that we delay this discussion until the morning. You have both forgotten your manners."

Taking a deep breath, Lord Angus nodded.

Prince Evnis said nothing. He stared at Elspeth, his gaze dark and intense.

Rhyan shivered at the strange hunger in his eyes.

"In any event," Lady Rose continued, "it would be impossible for Elspeth to leave tonight. She will require a few days to ready her things. We will *all* be able to discuss this more calmly and clearly after a night of rest."

The prince clenched his jaw. Without bowing to his hosts, he strode from the hall. His wife and son hurried after him.

"Our Uncle Evnis is a hard man," Elspeth cried as the door closed behind them.

"He is certainly ungentlemanly." Lady Rose reached across the table and grasped Elspeth's hand.

Rhyan agreed with both comments, but now that Prince Evnis was no longer in the room, her thoughts shifted.

I should be the one with the Dragon's Gift. *There must be some mistake. It must be me!*

FOUR

The Dragon's Gift

Elspeth wept while the fire crackled and sputtered in the hearth. Her sobs grated on Rhyan's nerves. Even with their aunt's comforting arm around her shoulders, her sister didn't stop. Her sniffles and low, distraught cries echoed in the dining hall.

A cruel lump of hot, jealous anger burned in Rhyan's chest. She couldn't bring herself to even look at her sister, let alone comfort her. She could hardly keep from shouting. *Why not me?*

"Why didn't you tell us he was our uncle?" Rhyan asked. "And why didn't you tell us that Elspeth has this...power?"

Lord Angus Kember sighed. "We hoped that Evnis would have his wish and discover a way to make the *Dragon's Gift* his own."

"What exactly is this *Gift*?" Rhyan asked.

"Long ago, an evil fell upon the Five Kingdoms." Lord Angus's deep voice carried over the snap and hiss of the fire and the continued drone of Elspeth's weeping. "Druin, a sorcerer and dragon-lord of extraordinary power, gathered a terrible army and set out to conquer Valles. We could not defeat him alone. One of the great wizards came to our aid. He used powerful magic to trap Druin in his dragon form, and he gifted the princes of Windover with the ability to renew the enchantment every ten years.

"From that day to this, that power—the *Dragon's Gift*—has been passed by blood to the firstborn of Windover. The princes even adopted a new surname to reflect their inherited gift: *Plendraig*, child of the dragon.

"Until the birth of your mother Branwen, the firstborn of Windover had always been a male—prince-to-be and holder of the *Gift*. Your grandfather was terribly troubled by the alteration that occurred with his own offspring. What should he do? Why hadn't his son the *Gift*? The old prince sought the advice of the wise for many years, until his days were ending. On his deathbed, he gave the title and lands to his son Evnis, although he could not change the fact that your mother bore the *Dragon's Gift*.

"Evnis hated her for it. When your grandfather died, Evnis sent your mother away, swearing he would find a means to make the power his own. Soon afterward, Branwen met my brother Dylan at the Southren Court. They were married that spring and the first few years passed happily for them. The birth of their two lovely daughters brought them great joy, and they decided to make a permanent home here at Caer Kember.

"When the time came to renew the enchantment, we all hoped that Evnis had fulfilled his wish, but it was not to be. He had sent messengers across the Eastren Sea but received no answer. He read through hundreds of ancient scrolls and books, but found no way to make the magic of the *Dragon's Gift* his own. Luckily, even in his anger and disgust, Evnis recognized that the enchantment must be renewed or the evil Druin would escape. So he sent for Branwen."

Lady Rose dabbed at Elspeth's tear-stained cheeks with a handkerchief. "I remember how happy she was to receive the message. Such a sweet soul! She hoped to reconcile with her brother and insisted that she and Dylan leave immediately for Windover Tor."

Lord Angus turned and gazed into the fire as if watching the events of the past unfold in the flames. "Branwen did not want to leave her babies," he added, "but you had both just gotten over the spotted fever and were still too weak to travel. You stayed with us while she and your father traveled to Windover. The enchantment was successfully renewed, but on the journey home...well, my dears..."

"We know what happened," Rhyan said. "Their carriage was blown off the Whyte Clyff Road and crashed on the rocks of the Westren Rapids!" The words spilled out like stones tumbling down the steep sides of those hateful cliffs. "We were left with you—and much good you have done us—hiding secrets! Allowing this bully to come in and tear the two of us apart! I can't—"

"Rhyan!" Elspeth cried out. "Do not be so cruel to Uncle Angus and Aunt Rose. They did their best for us. They gave us a home!" She burst into tears again.

As quickly as Rhyan's hot, frustrated anger had flared, her sister's tears extinguished the flame. "Elspeth is right," she whispered, moving to embrace her aunt and uncle in turn. "I'm so sorry, Aunt Rose...Uncle Angus."

Why did our parents have to die?

Lord Angus's eyes remained fixed on the fire. "This last year I've had much on my mind, with all the unrest across our lands. I've been distracted with worry about the corruption in the Southren Court, the raids and attacks reported near the Wastelands, and the tales of marauding beasts to the north. But I did not forget that the Time of Renewal was fast approaching and that the two of you were old enough to hear the truth and understand. I made up my mind to tell you many times. But I always lost my resolve at the thought of sending you to Windover with that hard-hearted prince.

"Evnis sent a message some weeks ago telling me he believed

he had found an answer that might allow Elspeth to remain here with us. But now…now he says he was mistaken."

Lord Angus faced his nieces. "Elspeth, I'm afraid that you will have to go. The enchantment must be renewed. I promise you I will convince Evnis that Caer Kember should continue to be your home, but for now you must go with him."

"Has anyone ever really seen a dragon?" Elspeth asked. "Nanny says monsters and faeries aren't real at all, but made up and put into stories to frighten children into behaving."

"I confess that in my desire to keep you safe, I have also kept you and Rhyan ignorant of much of the true history of our land," Lord Angus said. "I instructed those of our household to withhold certain knowledge and let you believe that all the ancient tales were mere make-believe. But the truth has, at last, found us, my dears. The sorcerer trapped beneath Windover Tor is all too real. I have read the accounts of those who were present when the last battle against Druin and his minions took place. You *must* go to Windover and renew the enchantment, or this ancient evil will be released into our world once again."

"Couldn't there be some mistake, Uncle?" Rhyan tried to keep her voice low. "Perhaps *I* have the *Gift.*" *I want it!*

Lord Angus shook his head. "I'm afraid there is no question, Rhyan. You are not firstborn. And there is another sure way to identify those who hold the *Dragon's Gift.* They always bear a certain physical trait—golden blonde hair."

Rhyan turned to look at her sister's carefully arranged yellow curls. Her own chestnut braid reflected the brown-red hair of the Prince of Windover.

"I can't believe this is happening to me," Elspeth said.

Rhyan's face grew hot. "You are such a baby, El. I would love to go. A dragon and magic! What excitement!"

"Of course!" Elspeth snapped. "You always think the stranger, the better, Rhyan."

"And what is that supposed to mean?"

"Precisely what it—"

"That is quite enough." Lady Rose stood and encouraged Elspeth to do the same. "We should all get some rest before we discuss this any further."

Lord Angus and Lady Rose left the hall with their arms around a still-sniffling Elspeth.

Rhyan trailed behind. She didn't want their empty comfort.

Later, in the darkness of her bedroom, she lay awake, staring into the shadows.

There must be a mistake. I am the one with the Gift! Man Lyr says I have power and talent. I can speak to birds! I know woodcraft and weather lore. I should be the one!

"Rhyan?" Elspeth whispered from across the room.

"Yes."

"Please don't be angry."

"I'm not, El."

Sheets rustled and then slippered feet shuffled across the cold stone floor.

The feather mattress sank as Elspeth sat on the edge of her bed. "I wish it was you, Rhyan. I don't want this. I'm afraid."

"Afraid?"

"You saw him. You heard his voice. He's so...cold." Elspeth sniffled.

Rhyan *had* seen and heard. Living with someone like that wouldn't be easy, even with a dragon and magic powers to keep one company. Elspeth would never be happy.

And what would it be like living here at Caer Kember without her?

"I shouldn't have called you a baby." She sat up and reached out in the darkness to pull her sister close. "I'm sorry."

Elspeth melted into her embrace and began to sob. "I'll miss you terribly. Don't let him take me away."

"Hush now. He can't keep us apart." Rhyan brushed back the tangled, tear-damp strands of Elspeth's hair. She remembered her uncle's words.

I'm afraid there is no question...the bearer of the Dragon's Gift *has always borne a certain physical trait—golden blonde hair.*

Rhyan fought to contain the jealous monster straining to break free inside her heart. *I am not like Evnis of Windover!* She hugged her sister tightly, so tightly. The rosewater scent of Elspeth's hair drove her envy away—at least for the moment.

"I'll talk to Uncle Angus in the morning. I'll make it right. You aren't going anywhere. If they insist, we'll smuggle out food and blankets and hide in the castle hedge maze. You know we're the only ones who have ever been able to find our way through it!"

"Yes." Elspeth laughed and then sniffled. "Dear Rhyan, I feel better now. Do you have a handkerchief?"

"I'm in my sleeping gown, Elspeth."

"Don't you keep one under your pillow?"

"No."

Elspeth sighed and got up. "But doesn't your pillow get wet when you cry?" Her feet whispered across the floor, back to her own bed.

Did Elspeth cry often? Why?

"El?"

"Yes?"

But she decided not to ask. The last thing she needed right now was more of her sister's tears. She'd talk to Elspeth about it in the morning.

"Sleep well."

"Sleep well, Rhyan."

FIVE

Missing

Rhyan's head echoed with the whispering of unfamiliar words. *'Pudorem taciturnitatis incurrere. Inter somno et somno mundi.'*

The strange chanting drummed against Rhyan's struggling consciousness. She swam in the dark toward the brighter surface of a deep pool, but the words kept pushing her back down toward the bottom.

'Silence...remain...between sleep and the dream world.'

It's too hard. I can't. Too tired...

"Rhyaaannnonn..." A familiar voice called her name.

She pushed away the drowning incantation and held on tight to the sound. The darkness lessened as she rose toward the surface.

"Rhyan? Rhyan, wake up dear." Lady Rose rubbed her niece's wrist.

"Aunt Rose...what?" Rhyan pried open her eyes and struggled to sit up on the bed.

"Thank the Crown! We've been trying to wake you for hours."

"What happened?" Rhyan looked around her bedchamber. The bright sunlight of midday streamed in the windows. A half dozen Watchguard stood at the door. They moved aside as the healer entered carrying a large, steaming bowl.

Tears welled up in Lady Rose's gentle eyes. "My dear child, I don't know how to tell you…it's Elspeth. She's been kidnapped."

"Kidnapped?" *I must still be dreaming.* "Why? Who?"

Lady Rose hesitated. "We can't be sure, but Prince Evnis of Windover is also missing. His lady says she woke this morning to find him gone. There's no sign of their carriage and driver, either."

"I don't understand." Rhyan's voice shook. She closed her eyes and pressed her palms against the throbbing heat of her eyelids. "I heard a voice and strange words. I felt trapped…"

"An evil potion, as sure as the sun rises, my lady," the healer said. "Your head is clouded with the power of it still." She held the bowl under Rhyan's chin, "Breathe deep now."

Rhyan gagged at the overpowering smell, but the rich, spicy tang of boiled herbs soon dispelled the mist from her thoughts.

"Has anyone gone after them?" She tossed off the coverlet and swung her legs out of bed. "How long has she been gone?"

"Go slowly, dear. Let the herbs complete their work." Lady Rose brushed a tangled curl away from her face. "Angus has taken his best men to Windover, but my worry is that Prince Evnis may not actually be the culprit. Whyever would he leave his wife and son behind?"

Remembering the way the prince had looked at his family last night, Rhyan didn't find it hard to imagine that he might abandon them.

"Let's get you feeling better before we talk anymore." Lady Rose stood. "Nanny will be here shortly to help you wash and dress. Then we'll get you something to eat."

Less than an hour later, Rhyan sat at one end of the servants'

table and choked down her breakfast. The warm bread and milk did nothing to untie the hard knots of worry that grew tighter and tighter in her stomach. It also didn't help that Nanny sat next to her, sobbing and dabbing at her eyes with a handkerchief while Cook paced the length of the long table.

But her mind did finally begin to clear, and a cold and frightening picture took shape.

Uncle Angus will not find Elspeth. The gates of Windover will be closed against him. I will never see her again. I'll be trapped here at Kember—a virtual prisoner to an ordinary existence! A powerless prisoner...

"I'm going out to the garden." She pushed her plate away.

Nanny Bess shook her head. "We're to keep you inside and out of harm's way," she said between sniffles.

"Couldn't the Watchguard accompany me? I simply need a bit of fresh air before I go back up to my room for a rest." She stifled a fake yawn.

Nanny considered a moment. "I'll send someone to Lady Rose for permission."

With her aunt's consent, Rhyan escaped from Nanny Bess, who never visited the garden because the flowers gave her uncontrollable sneezing fits.

"Thank the Crown!" Rhyan muttered under her breath as she walked down the long hallway with two Watchguard close on her heels.

Let Nanny cry in here. I need to act.

She pushed open the door and stepped out under the sky. She avoided looking at the hedge maze entrance, her heart twinging as she remembered her promise to Elspeth the previous night.

Entering the garden, she breathed the heady jumble of fragrances, but today the sweetness had a cloying finish, like a decomposing bouquet. Though the luscious colors still blazed summer bright, the blossoms drooped, exhausted, as if despair weighed them down. Rhyan looked toward the stone maiden, expecting to see tears on the cold cheeks, and caught sight of Old Llud. He sat on the farthest bench, amid his beloved lavender, his head bowed.

She joined him and waved the Watchguard away. The two men moved to stand at the garden entrance.

"Llud?"

Aged, bloodshot eyes brightened at the sight of his young friend. "Thank the Goddess that you at least are safe, my lady."

Rhyan glanced at the guards to be sure they remained out of earshot.

"I must go after her, Llud," she whispered. "I'm certain Man Lyr can help me, but I need to get to him. Aunt Rose has posted these Watchguard to attend to my safety and I doubt they will allow me to leave the castle grounds. But you once told me of a secret exit through the hedge maze. Can it still be used?"

The gardener glanced toward the stone maiden. "The danger would be too great. I cannot let you go, lady."

"Please, Llud! I promised Elspeth I would protect her. I must go."

Llud raised a shaking hand to his lined forehead. "Would that I were younger..." He took a deep breath. "I will help you, Lady Rhyannon. But you must take something of mine along to protect you."

"Anything you ask, Llud. What is it?"

"My grandson, Collen."

"Your grandson!" Rhyan burst out.

One of the Watchguard took a step in their direction.

Cursing to herself, Rhyan lowered her voice. "I'm sorry, but that would be impossible. It will be difficult enough for me to get out of here alone without being noticed."

Old Llud turned to face her. "There is an Evil about, my lady! I feel it in my bones. That storm yesterday was the Goddess trying to defend her land from hurt...but she fades with the years. People have forgotten her. Who can help us now? I am old, too old. I cannot go with you myself, but neither can I let you go alone. Collen will see you safe. He's a bright lad and steady. Good at forestcraft, too. He's just come over from Rivertown to help me this day. Be a wise girl and say you'll take him, or I'll not show you the secret door."

Rhyan opened her mouth to argue, but something in her old friend's face stopped her. "I will take him," she whispered.

The gardener gave her a wink. "I always thought you were a lass as could know a good bargain, my lady. Come back in an hour. I'll meet you at the entrance of the hedge maze and see you to the secret exit. Collen will be awaitin' you on the outside."

An hour later, Nanny Bess slept, mouth open and snoring, in the corner chair in Rhyan's bedroom.

Careful to make as little sound as possible, Rhyan plumped up the pillows on her bed and tucked the sheets in around them, creating the illusion of a body beneath the covers.

Perfect. None of the chambermaids will dare disturb my sleep. She shrugged off a mild pang of guilt that Nanny would probably be the one to discover she had gone.

Her heart pounded like a message drum as she slipped out of the bedroom and eased the door closed. If they caught her now, she'd likely never get another chance. She half-ran down the servants' stairs and through the back hall in her stockinged feet, only slipping into her heavy traveling boots when she reached the garden door. She imagined approaching steps as she tied the laces, but when she looked back the hall was empty.

True to his word, Old Llud waited at the entrance to the maze. After a quick glance to the door, Rhyan followed him under the arch and down the dense shrub-walled pathways.

Precious minutes ticked by as they navigated the corridors of the maze, past stone walls, animal statues, and silvered mirrors. Instead of taking the double-turn that led to the center lookout, from which the entire maze could be viewed, Llud led her down one of the dead-end paths. When they reached what appeared to be another impenetrable wall of thick, spiny greenery, Llud smiled, then slipped into the bushes as if nothing stood in his way.

Rhyan approached and reached out her hand.

Where was the opening?

Llud's hand reached out of the greenery, grasped hers, and pulled her through.

They stood together in a small space between the border of the maze and the tall outer stone wall of the castle grounds. The branches of the maze arched over their heads. A little sunlight filtered through, but they were hidden from the view of anyone on the wall.

"A bit of a diagonal cut to hide the opening from maze-goers," Llud said. "It's an old secret, one I've kept to myself over the years."

He put his shoulder against a large vertical stone in the wall and pushed. The rock fell outward, hitting the ground with a grass-muffled thump.

"Collen?" the old gardener whispered.

"Here, Grandad." A face appeared in the gap and Collen greeted Rhyan with a wide smile. His full head of curly black hair framed eyes the same deep brown as his grandfather's.

A hand gripped Rhyan's shoulder. "Lady Rhyannon?"

She bit her lip, silently cursing as she reopened the wound she'd given herself at dinner the previous night, and spun around.

It was the Prince of Windover's son.

"What are you doing here?"

"Take me with you," Hale demanded.

"I most certainly will not!" Rhyan responded in a loud voice.

"Sshh!" Collen and his grandfather said at the same time.

"Why would I take you with me?" Rhyan whispered. "Your father kidnapped my sister."

"He did not! I know it. I want to prove his innocence. You must take me." The boy stomped his foot. "If you don't, I'll yell out to the guard as loudly as I can. You'll never get away."

Rhyan clenched her hands into fists. *What an infant.* "You aren't old enough to go! And you're dressed as if you were attending a dancing party." She pointed to his black silk, silver-trimmed shirt.

Old Llud settled things. "Here now! None of that, my lady. I think the young man should go with you." He waved off Rhyan's protest. "What's your name, young sir?"

The boy bowed. "I am Hale Evnis Plendraig, heir to the Prince of Windover, and I am old enough to stand up for the honor of my family, sir. I am the same age as my *fair* cousins." He glowered. "In fact, I am six moons older."

It surprised Rhyan that he was her own age. Young men petitioned to join the Watchguard at fourteen turnings, but her cousin didn't look as if he had the strength to hold up a heavy Watchshield long enough to block a single blow.

"I'm honored to meet you, Master Hale." Llud bowed in return. "You seem a young gentleman well-grown to these old eyes. If you go with my lady Rhyannon, there must be a promise from you to aid and protect her on her journey. Have you courage? For the questing may be dangerous and the journey long. Being a noble man of honor, I believe you will keep this promise. What say you?"

Hale thrust his chin upwards and glared at Rhyan. "I give my word. The men of Windover *are* men of honor."

"Through the hole with you then. Collen'll give you a hand."

"No, Llud. I will not take him with me!"

"It is out of our hands, lady," Llud said. "Young Hale has his own heart-quest to follow. He is your kinsman and deserves your trust until he proves unworthy."

Sighing, Rhyan nodded as the boy stepped into the opening. Then she hugged the old gardener hard. "Thank you," she whispered.

Llud brushed away tears. "I've told Collen to wait a bit behind the rose hedge while I raise a false alarm on the other side of the grounds. Young Kendall, the newest of the Guard, is the Daywatch on this wall. He's a rash lad and loves his sword. I've no doubt he'll be runnin' off to find the fightin' as soon as the Danger Bell sounds. Keep your eyes on him. When he turns his back, be off as quick as you can."

The opening was a tight fit, but Collen grasped Rhyan's hand and pulled her out into the meadow. Gold-green grasses swayed in the light breeze. Just a few feet away stood the tall, wild rose hedge where they were to wait. The warm, sweet scent of the pink blossoms hung in the air, reminding her of Elspeth.

She turned back toward the wall and smiled at Llud's worried face.

He reached through and squeezed her hand one last time. "Come home safe, lady. And bring her back."

"I will."

SIX

The Call

I am free!

Rhyan's heart pounded as she ran beneath the leaves of Eldon Wood. Collen kept pace, stepping among the tree roots and fallen branches with the deft surety of long practice. Twice, Hale stumbled behind them, but the princeling got up unassisted each time, waving at them to continue.

The clanging Danger Bell and shouts from the Watchguard in response to Llud's false alarm muted when they entered the forest. As they followed the path to Man Lyr's house, Rhyan prayed their escape had gone unnoticed.

The old man waited at the door of the stone cottage as if he expected them.

"Kara Falcon brought me the tidings from Caer Kember and beyond." He glanced at the bird perched in the rowan tree beside his front door. "I know of Elspeth's disappearance. We are all in great danger. Greater than ever I could have imagined, although the signs of it have been there to read these many months."

"What do you mean, sir?" Rhyan asked.

"Come inside. I will tell what I have learned."

Packs and supplies lay scattered about the cottage floor. Man Lyr motioned them toward the hearth table. He poured out mugs of cider.

"The evil one beneath Windover Tor is awake," he began.

"Uncle Angus spoke of him," Rhyan said. "He told us he had brought an army against Valles long ago, but was defeated by a wizard—trapped by magic."

Man Lyr nodded. "Druin Canwyr is truly wicked and vile. He is a dragon-lord and renegade wizard of extraordinary power who once terrorized these lands. He believed wizard-kind was the superior race and that they should rule all: humans, Faeries, giants, the sentient beasts, Tree Walkers—everyone. The humans banded together to fight, but they had little hope. Over the centuries, they had lost touch with the land magic—their only true power and the ancient gift of the Goddess. Without it, they could not stand against Druin.

"He enslaved those who came to him and pled mercy, subjecting them to the worst possible dark magic—a corruption of their very natures. Trust, order, and respect gave way to suspicion and chaos...and a deep hatred of all those who did not follow Druin's path. In desperation, those who still held true sent word to the far-off Isle of Wyde."

"To the Wizard's Council!" Rhyan had always been fascinated by her tutor's stories of the mages who had once lived among the people of Valles.

Man Lyr nodded. "The wizards felt responsible for the renegade Druin. They sent one of their own to help—Mannawyddan the White Wizard. He cast a spell over the dragon-lord and trapped him in his beastly shape, confining him in the ancient labyrinth beneath Windover Tor. Mannawyddan bound the spell that held the evil one with the blood of the Prince of Windover. He charged the prince and his heirs with the responsibility of using their power to renew the enchantment every ten years."

"My family has always done their duty," Hale said.

"They have in the past, young lord, they have indeed. However, through Kara Falcon, I received word that the enchantment of the White Wizard," Man Lyr paused and took a quick sip from his mug, "has weakened. Somehow the dragon-lord has regained access to a portion of his magic. His power grows daily."

Hale paled. "But it is nearly the Time of Renewal."

"It is," Man Lyr said. "And if the weakened enchantment is not renewed, Druin will be released from his dragon form and his stone prison. He will once again wreak havoc across the Five Kingdoms."

Rhyan's jaw tightened. "That's why Elspeth has been taken—because she bears the *Dragon's Gift*."

"Yes," Man Lyr said.

"Did you always know of Elspeth's...birthright?" she asked.

Man Lyr nodded.

Why am I not the one? Did you not say I have enchanted blood? Rhyan tried to swallow her jealousy. "Why didn't you tell me? Why didn't you teach me more about our true history?"

"Your Nanny wasn't just following Lord Angus's orders when she taught you that dragons and faeries weren't real," Man Lyr said. "She is one of the many who have truly forgotten. These peaceful times have caused the history of the Age of Wizards and the secrets to the Goddess's prismed path to become naught but a collection of children's tales to be told by the fire on a cold evening. In recent years, those in Kember who have spoken out for the old ways and beliefs have found themselves shunned and vilified as heathens." He met Rhyan's gaze. "Because of your love for the outdoors, your uncle asked me to teach you of the natural world. I had to proceed carefully with other aspects of your education, or risk losing that privilege."

"My grandsire is one who follows the Goddess's way, sir,"

Collen said. "He taught my pa and me but told us to keep secret his words or risk the hatred of others, as you say."

"Enough history." Prince Evnis's haughty manner echoed in Hale's demanding tone. "I must find my father!"

"I'm *quite* certain my sister and your father will be together," Rhyan said.

"Exactly what do you mean by that, cousin?"

"Precisely what you have assumed I mean, *dear* cousin."

"If you were a man I would claim insult!" Hale put a hand to his belt knife.

"I am the match of any man." Rhyan slammed her clay mug on the table, breaking the handle.

"Enough!" Man Lyr shouted. He held up a long-fingered hand. His dark gray cloak billowed as if caught in a gust of phantom wind. His eyes flashed. "Put aside your petty arguments! Would you risk so much?"

Rhyan's breath caught in her throat. "I beg pardon, sir," she whispered.

"And I," Hale muttered.

"Now, I have prepared provisions and supplies," Man Lyr said. "Each of you must carry a small pack. My pony will bear the rest.

"Rhyan, I give you this weapon." He handed her a short, curved blade in a leather scabbard, embossed with a circular symbol of twisted lines. "It was mine in my youth. I hope you will not have occasion to use it, but I fear you may and, when you do, let it be done with great care. Do not let emotions rule your actions."

Rhyan bowed her head as she tied the scabbard to her belt. *He thinks me a child still.*

"Where are we going, sir?" Collen asked.

"You three must go in search of a talisman that will give us the power we need to face Druin."

"But what of my father?" Hale asked.

"He can only be saved by Druin's defeat."

"Where are *you* going?" Rhyan asked.

"I must consult an old friend who has long studied the blood-binding spells of the wizards, as well as the ancient powers of the Goddess. She may have knowledge that will assist us in this trial. And I will attempt to draw near enough to Windover Tor that I may determine the true state of the enchantment and the growth of Druin's power. I will meet with you as soon as I am able."

"Do not send me away on some safe errand while you go to fight this evil!" Rhyan argued. "I am strong! I want to find my sister and save her from this dragon. I want—"

"Rhyannon!" Man Lyr's gray gaze pierced like an icy wind. "The *Dragon's Gift* is failing. Only the talisman holds the power to destroy Druin. Your sister will be but the first to feel the dragon-lord's wrath once he is freed from beneath the Tor. Countless lives will be lost. We must have the talisman—do you understand?"

"I understand, sir." She again bowed her head. *Curse my temper!*

"A fortnight past I found reference to the talisman in an ancient manuscript," Man Lyr told them. "It is in the keeping of the Kirrin, the ancient guardian of the Old Forest."

The Old Forest! No one dared enter that sacred realm of the Faerie.

"The forest lies southwest, across the River Briden," Rhyan said. "I remember our study of maps."

Man Lyr nodded. "Our lessons will serve you well on this journey."

"How will I find the Faerie once we reach the Old Forest?"

"I will send Kara Falcon ahead with a message," Man Lyr said. "The Faerie will meet you and guide you to the guardian—and the talisman. It is written that the Kirrin will only release it to one who has the inner power and strength to use it."

Pinpricks of excitement spread down Rhyan's arms. *It must be me! It has to be.*

"Be wise while among the Faerie, Little Dragon. Remember the lore I have taught you. Do not insult them. Be courteous, but cautious."

Collen cleared his throat. "Beg pardon, wise sir, but won't the faeries steal us away like they did those southren village children last autumn?"

Man Lyr patted the young man's shoulder. "I am not sending you to see the wicked spirits that are no doubt in league with our enemy, Collen, but rather *The* Faerie. The Faerie of the Old Forest are as noble and fair a people as you will ever meet. They are, however, somewhat over-proud, with many customs which may seem strange to you. That is why I give you this advice—offer no insult, act with courtesy, but also with caution. They are our best allies against Druin and we must remain on good terms."

Collen nodded.

"You should leave immediately. Stay under the cover of Eldon Wood as you head for the river. Find Heart's Crossing—it is just north of the Eastren Rapids. You will know the place by a large stone of red granite, fixed like a pillar on the sand near an ancient pier. An old friend of mine is the ferryman at the Crossing. He is called Keven of Tralleigh. When he asks what fare you can pay, tell him that I have sent you and say this:

Fair Tribute only can we pay
To one who loves the Lady Bride.
Tell us what you will, my friend
Once we reach the other side.

Man Lyr made Rhyan recite the verse until she repeated it without error.

Kara Falcon's angry cry sounded outside. Man Lyr hurried to the door. The falcon landed on the ground clutching a large raven in her talons.

"Look!" Collen pointed skyward. A second raven winged its way north.

"There is no time to lose," Man Lyr said. "You must hurry on your way before the messenger reports to his master."

Rhyan shivered. Only yesterday she had been playing a game with Elspeth in this forest. Now darkness and danger lurked everywhere.

SEVEN

Heart's Crossing

Rhyan found it odd that an animal born and raised in the forest should prove skittish at the sound of calling birds and rustling leaves. But, odd or not, these sounds spooked Beck the pony. They walked for hours before the pack horse settled into a steady pace. Just as Rhyan sighed in frustrated relief, Collen called a halt.

"Why are we stopping?" she asked.

"Just a short rest, lady." Collen gave a nod toward Hale still struggling down the path toward them. "A wee catch of our breaths might not go amiss."

Rhyan clenched her teeth. At this pace they would never reach the river today. Why, *why* had she let herself be talked into bringing this soft nursery lord along? If they didn't reach Heart's Crossing soon, Uncle Angus's men might catch up and force them to return to Caer Kember. She'd never find the talisman...or rescue Elspeth.

"Don't worry, lady. We'll be to the River Briden before sunset."

"Are you certain, Collen?"

"Aye, sure and certain. It won't hurt to give your cousin a minute or two."

Hale Plendraig looked far less than princely as he puffed up beside the pack pony.

"Are we going too fast for you, cousin?" Rhyan coated her voice in sugar.

"No," Hale answered. "I was ill last month, that's all. My strength hasn't fully returned."

Rhyan laughed.

Hale clenched his fists at his side.

"Water, my lord?" Collen offered.

"Yes, thank you."

As Hale drank, Rhyan caught Collen's disappointed gaze.

She blushed and turned away. *It isn't my fault! No one could have patience with such a pampered princeling.*

Collen took the water skin and refastened it to the pony's pack. "When you've rested a bit, we'll go on, my lord."

"I'm ready."

"We've time to catch our—"

"I said I'm ready, Collen. Proceed."

"Aye, my lord."

The path grew rougher and rounded river stones marked its curves. The sound of rushing water announced the river's presence long before they emerged from under the forest canopy, just where the River Trall met the Briden in the tumble of the Eastren Rapids.

"It's beautiful, my lady," Collen breathed.

Rhyan nodded. The jewel-blue sky reflected on the water's surface. Glittering and foaming, the current flowed past slick, deep red stones, creating a startling contrast of brilliant color.

She could never look at rough river waters without thinking of her parents and how they died. The rapids taunted and laughed at her. They questioned and threatened.

How different life might have been if they had safely returned from their trip to Windover Tor.

Hale lumbered out of the woods to stand next to Collen.

"The Crossing is just north. Let's keep moving." Rhyan hoisted her pack and took the lead. She set off, following the river.

The sun shone, fierce and bright, midway through its descent of the westren sky. Soon it would disappear behind the towering oaks of the Old Forest. Sweat trickled between her shoulder blades.

Collen's sudden, urgent whisper in her ear made Rhyan jump. "Keep walking, lady."

"What's wrong?"

"Don't look 'round. I think we're being followed."

"Uncle Angus's guards?"

"I think not. Your uncle's men would have declared themselves to us right away. And Beck seems more afraid than nervous now—skittering as if he smells danger behind us."

"Who, then?"

"I don't know, lady. You take Beck's lead and I'll fall back to the rear. If you hear me shout, run on to Heart's Crossing."

"But, Collen—"

"Beg pardon, lady, but we don't have time for a discussion."

Rhyan couldn't help smiling. Trust Collen to politely tell her to close her mouth and do as she was told.

"Be careful, though, Collen. Will you please?"

A flush spread across his brown cheeks. "I will, lady."

Collen jogged a few paces back and Hale came up to walk beside Rhyan. As they continued, a bird flew across the path. Beck shied and bumped into the young heir of Windover, nearly knocking him down.

"That pony is more trouble than he's worth!" Hale rubbed his shoulder.

"He's not the only one," Rhyan mumbled.

"Pardon?"

"Nothing, cousin."

"Who do you think these Faerie really are?" Hale asked.

"Whatever are you talking about?"

"The Faerie-people that your hermit friend has sent us to meet. Are they some forgotten tribe of wood-dwellers? Are you certain they aren't hostile? Can we trust your Man Lyr?"

Rhyan wiped the sweat from her forehead, but kept walking. Her own breath now came as ragged as Hale's. Every muscle strained as she anticipated Collen's warning cry.

She had no energy to argue. "I believe everything Man Lyr told us. He would never knowingly send me into danger. He is a fine and honorable man, hermit or not."

"So you say," Hale countered.

"Stones and bones, Hale! Yes, I do say! Can you not—"

Collen's shout burst out behind them.

"Run!"

Hale looked back. "Whatever is the matter?"

"Run!" Rhyan yelled, pushing her cousin forward.

Beck pulled hard at his tether as a blood-curdling howl sounded behind them.

Wolves!

"It can't be!" Hale said in an odd, strangled voice.

Rhyan ran on, straining for a glimpse of the pillar that marked Heart's Crossing.

Collen sprinted up beside them and took the pony's lead. "They're some distance back but gaining. They'll catch us if we don't reach the crossing soon."

Running on, they rounded a copse of evergreens and the standing stone loomed up before them. Twice a man's height and hewn from deep, blood-red granite, it stood, solid and ancient, on the riverbank. Just beyond, a wide-bottomed boat floated, moored to a short wooden dock.

A scarlet-robed man reclined in the boat, a long pipe in his mouth. He did not move as Hale and Rhyan tumbled aboard and collapsed gasping at his feet. Collen stood on shore with Beck. The pony balked and refused to step aboard the vessel.

"Keven of Tralleigh?" Rhyan's breath caught on the question and she coughed.

"Aye." The boatkeeper never looked up from beneath his wide-brimmed hat.

"We must cross the river," Hale said, as Rhyan struggled to stop coughing.

"Indeed," Keven of Tralleigh puffed on his pipe. "And what business would three young adventurers have in the Old Forest, I'm wondering?"

Hale's face burned red. "You buffoon! Can you not hear that wolves are chasing us? Get us across the river!"

Keven sat up and lifted the brim of his hat. Brown eyes twinkled as he leaned toward Hale and lifted a feathery eyebrow. "Is that so, young master? And what fare will you pay this humble buffoon to ferry you across the River Briden?"

"Fare!" Hale shouted. "Do you—"

"Silence, you imbecile!" Rhyan broke in, finally able to speak. "Keven of Tralleigh, I speak these words to you as Man Lyr instructed me:

> *Fair Tribute only can we pay*
> *To one who loves the Lady Bride.*
> *Tell us what you would, my friend*
> *Once we reach the other side.*"

The ferryman stood up and stretched. "Man Lyr? Well, we shall speak on this later. You have offered fair payment for my services. When would you like to depart?"

"Now!" Hale and Rhyan shouted.

"Please, sir," Rhyan added.

"As you wish." Keven bowed.

"Beg pardon, lady," Collen said. "I'll need some help with poor Beck. He can't seem to decide which he's more afraid of, the wolves or the water."

"Let me assist you." Keven reached out two fingers and gently touched the pony between the eyes. "Come aboard, Master Beck, be at peace."

Beck gave a soft nicker that sounded like an apology and stepped into the boat. Once Collen climbed aboard, the ferryman tapped his pipe against an elaborate heart carved into the prow and the boat left the shore. Without oars or a sail, the vessel moved across the water. The River Briden flowed swift and strong, but the boat traveled a sure, straight line.

"What powers your boat, sir?" Collen asked.

"Not the time for long tales now, boy," Keven answered.

A fierce howling followed the ferryman's boat across the river. Rhyan looked back in time to see a dozen black wolves emerge from the trees and stop at the riverbank near the Heart Stone. The huge, snarling beasts towered almost half the height of the red granite pillar.

"Am I feverish, or are those wolves larger than they ought to be?" she asked.

Keven of Tralleigh puffed hard on his pipe before answering her question. "Do not fear for your health, lady, those beasts are most certainly quite enormous." He turned toward Hale. "But then, the northren variety are somewhat larger than their southren cousins, are they not, young master?"

The prince's son pressed his lips together and looked away.

Why would Hale know anything about these wolves?

"Look!" Collen pointed.

The wolves stopped howling and parted ranks as a horseman appeared from beneath the eaves of Eldon Wood. Mounted on a black stallion, the armored figure wore a dark chainmail hauberk and coif accented with bright red.

He rode to the edge of the river. As he raised a gleaming black sword in challenge, three ebon jewels adorning the blade glimmered and writhed as if alive.

The sky darkened, and the sounds of the river muted. A hungry tendril of evil reached across the water and gripped Rhyan's heart. She held her breath as the rider lifted his shield. It bore a red dragon on a midnight field.

"Back!" Keven shouted. "You cannot cross the River Briden!

Back to your master, evil one."

His command released the invisible noose around Rhyan's heart. Relief flooded through her as the sunlight and the sounds of the river returned.

The dark knight held his position for a few long moments. His eyes met Rhyan's across the water and she heard his voice as if he stood right beside her.

"You are one of us, golden-eyed dragon-child."

Then, his mount rearing, the knight barked a harsh order to the wolves. Yipping and howling, they followed him back into Eldon Wood.

"No," Rhyan whispered.

"What is it, my lady?" Collen asked.

"The knight spoke to me—didn't you hear him?"

"I heard nothing but the growling and barking of the wolves," Collen said. "My Lord Hale, did you hear the knight speak?"

"No," Hale answered, still sullen.

"What did he say, my lady?" Collen asked.

"Nothing...perhaps I imagined it." But she knew she had not. *You are one of us, golden-eyed dragon-child.*

Finally, the boat reached the opposite bank. The massive trunks of the Old Forest's ancient trees stood a mere hundred paces from the water's edge. As Rhyan stepped from the boat, they loomed over her, like giant guardians awaiting her challenge.

A sudden weariness weighed down her arms and legs. "I need to rest," she said.

"Come and share my evening meal," said Keven of Tralleigh. "I am wondering why the Dark Knight of Cumbria pursues three young travelers, and there is also the matter of your fare, as agreed."

"Thank you, sir," Rhyan said. "I am Rhyan Kember, niece of Lord Angus Kember. This is my cousin, Hale Plendraig, son of the Prince of Windover, and our friend and companion, Collen,

William's son. We accept your kind offer."

Keven's house stood at the edge of the Old Forest. Built of round river stones and roofed with thick, moldering grass thatching, the simple, one-story building appeared as ancient as the wood it bordered.

Pulling aside the heavy door tapestry, Keven motioned for them to enter. They gratefully sat on chairs fashioned from boulders and padded with down cushions. The seats ranged around a table made from a sturdy rock topped with a round, flat stone. Strange, blackish bricks burned in a red granite fireplace built into the far wall.

When they commented on his unique furnishings, Keven smiled. "No wood here, my young friends. Even my fire is fueled by peat bricks I purchase from eastren bog farmers. I live under the eaves of temperamental trees, you see. They wouldn't take kindly to such proof of the treacherous murders of their kin."

Keven served them cool spring water in ornate metal mugs and an earthy-tasting tuber stew in clay bowls filled from the cauldron hung over the fire.

"Thank you again, sir," Rhyan said. "Your stew is delicious."

"You will hear me better with full stomachs. The time has come to pay your fare and listen to my tale."

Rhyan closed her eyes as the singsong voice of their host began his story.

EIGHT

Keven's Tale

"Long, long ago—before the Derran lords built their great castles and before the mountain Garanth spewed molten rock to blanket the Faerie island of Leas—the Westren lands knew two ruling families, the Dalrians and the Trallendon.

"To the North lived the Dalrians. Cold and fierce they were, and yet beautiful, with skin and hair as white as mountain ice. They ruled their harsh land with proud strength. But conceit and the belief in the superiority of their race led to a deep disdain of all others.

"Southward lived the Trallendon. Warm as the Dalrians were cold, the Trallendon were a bright and laughing people—if also somewhat wary of outsiders. Poets, minstrels, and bards were revered by their nation. The High Court at Tralleigh held a never-ending, glittering succession of balls and masques. The gardens at court had no equal, for the Trallendon were friends to the forest and the river, and they let their gardens grow in a wild, natural way that mirrored their rambling, flamboyant hearts.

"For a thousand years, the two families kept apart. Never was the Ice River crossed.

"Then, one Spring, a son of the Trallendon, the youngest of the royal house, made up his mind to leave his people. He sought not freedom so much as a glimpse of the wider world. He wanted to set foot in hidden places and hear new voices and stories.

"He was a thoughtful youth, you see, who had always felt out of place among his family. Although something of the poet, the bard, and the philosopher lived in him, there was not enough of any one thing to make him content to choose a set path for himself. As he grew, his dreams of adventure and escape began to consume his waking and sleeping thoughts. And his family wondered greatly about him. They spoke of him in whispers behind their hands. What would become of him?

"So, one day, the young lord set out on his own. He meant to travel to the Ice River and then north into the Westren Mountains. He wished to find the Path of Sorrow; the mountain pass that had brought his ancestors to this land after they had escaped the destruction of their own. Were the old lands still desolate? Had life returned? Did new peoples walk there?

"His family bid him farewell. They shook their heads. They did not understand the spirit of adventure that called to him.

"For many days, he traveled with only the frigid wind as a companion. Then, on a night when the moon showed her full face, he heard singing. The lonely, searching melody floated across the river and took hold of his soul. Like a madman, he jumped into the frigid waters of the Ice River to follow the siren call.

"The chill fingers of the deadly current shocked him back to awareness. They clawed at him, stripping away his lifeforce. He lost feeling in his legs and his heart thumped in distress. Gasping for air, he called out to the singer, 'Hear me! Help me!'

"In answer to his cry, the song changed. The words became strong with command. Suddenly, a wondrous thing happened.

Instead of pulling him down, the waters of the Ice River bore him up. They carried him to the rime-encrusted northren bank. Strong hands reached down and pulled him out of danger.

"The son of the Trallendon opened his eyes and beheld the fairest maiden he had ever seen. Her hair was lily-white, her eyes the sharp blue of a winter sky, and her skin as pale as new cream.

"He stammered out his name and his thanks.

"'I saved you only on a whim.' Her voice sent a chill through the young man's soul. Cold, it was—cold as the waters from which the young man had so recently found his escape. 'I am Bridelyn, daughter of Nellan of Dalria. Why do you trespass on our lands, Southrener?'

"'Why, it was you who pulled me onto your lands, fair one. If you wished to deny me passage, perhaps it would be best if you pushed me back into the river.'

"Bridelyn of Dalria threw back her head and laughed.

"So began the downfall of the kingdoms of Dalria and Tralleigh.

"Months passed. As they traveled together along the banks of the Ice River and up to Mount Teldar and back, the maiden and the adventurer realized that they shared love. Not the sugary, flowery, spring-love of youth, but a deep, powerful knowledge that their souls were bound together in an eternal bond.

"'We must marry,' Bridelyn insisted.

"'Your family will not be pleased.'

"'Let us go together to Rath Dalria.' Bridelyn refused to relent. 'Let us stand and meet their arguments. Our courage will prove us.'

"The son of the Trallendon hated conflict above all. 'I would not have my first meeting with your family be a quarrel. I will wait for you here. Approach your father privately. Send word once he gives his approval.'

"At the ancient *Teorainn* Bridge, where the Ice River is born, the young adventurer and his beloved reluctantly parted.

"Hidden in the shadow of Mount Teldar, a lone rider watched the couple make their farewell. It was Brastyn, heir of Dalria and brother to Bridelyn. He waited until his sister traveled out of sight and then galloped across the bridge in pursuit of the son of the Trallendon. Armed and angry, he confronted his sister's suitor.

"'Bridelyn would never marry one as lowly as you.' He spat on the ground to show his scorn. "You have ensorcelled her.'

"'She loves me as I love her,' the adventurer insisted.

"When you are dead, your spell will break." Brastyn drew his sword.

"The son of the Trallendon was unarmed. He raised his hands and stepped back. But from the nearby wood came the high-pitched hum of arrows slicing through the chill air.

"In an instant, Brastyn of Dalria lay dead on the ground. Trallendon archers, hunting in the forest, had seen the stranger draw steel against a son of the royal house. The penalty for such an action was death.

"A bloody and terrible war broke out. The fighting went on for years until most of the Trallendon and Dalrians forgot the death that had begun the conflict and remembered only their hatred of each other.

"Finally, only one member of each royal house was left alive: The princess and leader of the Dalrian army, and the youngest son of Trallendon who still refused to fight. Each knew that the killing would continue until their two peoples destroyed each other. In final desperation, they met again on the *Teorainn* Bridge.

"'Your hair still glows as snow under the moon's fullness,' he told her.

"'And your tongue is still as silver as the Crown of Teldar.' Bitterness edged her words with ice.

"'Bridelyn, we must stop the fighting.' He moved closer.

"She held up a hand, her expression as cold and emotionless

as a frozen lake. 'Do not approach me, you who have never fought, even to save your own family. I agree that the fighting must end. There is a way, a terrible way. I will renounce my claim to Dalria and leave my guard captain as steward to the kingdom. He has no blood power but is a proud and honorable man. He will lead my people to the future.'

"'The fighting will continue.'

"'No,' Bridelyn said. 'I have found a way to bind the river so that none of our two races may cross without my permission. I shall protect my people through my sacrifice.'

"'Sacrifice? Will you use *blood* power?' The Trallendon asked.

"'I will cast a powerful enchantment.' She looked away.

"'Bridelyn! What price will you pay for this magic? I still love you! Do not let us be parted forever. If you ever loved me, let me share this task with you.' Again, he moved toward her.

"'Touch me not!' she commanded. 'We share the fault for this wretched war. This leeching love has made nothing but death. And yet....' Her eyes grew as empty as a wasteland. 'Perhaps it is right that I share the price with you. Yes! Yes, we shall pay for our sins together! I speak the words to bind us both—

As my soul shall be one with the water
I command yours shall need mine within sight.
Touch me not! Lest your breath
Be stolen by Death!
The Rivers will hold you—
Protect you but bind you!
Till my word release you.
Beware! Be bound! Beware!'

"As she uttered the final, compelling words of the vow, Bridelyn dove from the bridge into the rushing waters of the Ice River. The son of the Trallendon moved to jump in after her, but found his feet held fast by the spell. He cried aloud as the frigid torrent of water swirled into a whirlpool around Bridelyn's body. Gasping, he fell to his knees, forced to watch as magic-made ice fingers tore away his beloved's clothing, her hair, her skin, and even her bones. But, although she disappeared into the depths, the son of the Trallendon knew that his love was not truly dead. For he could feel her soul—alive and suffering—in the water.

"To this day, Bridelyn protects her people and allows no enemy to cross the Ice River—now the River Briden—or its tributaries. The Steward and his people have prospered even without the proud blood power of their lost royalty. Rath Dalria is no longer the fort of the Winter Sun but is now named Rath Mormar—fort of the Royal Steward.

"The son of the Trallendon also lives on. The last of his people died more than four hundred years ago. He lives on alone... and waiting. Regretting his choices with every setting of the sun."

Keven sighed and looked up from the dying fire. "I am he. I am Keven Tralleigh, last son of the royal house of Trallendon."

NINE

The Faerie

The soft caress of morning's first light streamed through a small window in Keven's stone cottage, urging Rhyan awake. Stepping over sleeping bodies, she crept out the tapestry door. A clear dawn sky brightened overhead, but thick mist hung low over the murmuring river. As she approached the bank, a foggy cloak enveloped her.

Disjointed thoughts filled her head: Elspeth, her uncle, the giant wolves, and the strange tale of Keven Tralleigh.

As she recalled Keven's story, the voice of the river sharpened. The tumble of the water formed almost-words. Rhyan strained to hear the message.

It feels like...a warning.

"She seems rather troubled this day."

Rhyan spun to find Keven standing close behind her.

"You startled me!"

"My pardon, Lady Rhyan. I woke and found you missing."

"I felt uneasy and didn't wish to disturb anyone," she said. "I hoped a walk might help to clear my head, but the river...spoke."

"I understand." Keven gazed out over the water. "The voice of the river often calls to me when I am unsettled in mind and soul. Beware of her, my newfound friend. The river speaks with Bridelyn's voice and she is—even at her best—cold-hearted. Always be cautious near her banks, for she has grown empty and cruel over the centuries." He sighed and seemed to shake himself. "Come back with me now, before your friends wake and miss you."

Rhyan turned from the riverbank with Keven, but a sudden chill brushed across her shoulders like the touch of an icy hand. She stopped and looked back toward the water.

Keven grasped her hand and pulled her onward. "Bridelyn's farewell. Let us hurry."

The warmth of the cottage dispelled the chill.

"Good morn, my lady." Collen greeted her with a bright smile.

"Good morn, Collen. And to you, cousin."

Hale nodded but did not meet Rhyan's eyes.

I do not trust him.

"Keven." She watched Hale closely. "Who was that knight pursuing us yesterday? You gave him a name."

"The Dark Knight of Cumbria was a great warrior once—a hero from a distant land," Keven said. "I heard tales of him long ago at my grandsire's knee."

Hale did not react to Keven's answer.

Perhaps I am wrong.

"I know those stories." Collen drew near. "The knight came to the Five Kingdoms of Valles in search of a purpose—a path— a life of meaning. King Daffyd, the last crowned king of Kember, offered him a place as captain of his Sentinel Guard, the protectors of the land. Under the knight's leadership, the Guard gained great renown by hunting down fell beasts that menaced the outskirts of the kingdom. After many years, the knight retired from the king's service, married a maiden, and had a child—a son, I think.

"The final story tells how, one year, King Daffyd asked if the knight would come out of retirement and escort his eldest daughter to the kingdom of her betrothed on the eastren coast.

"The knight did as he was asked but, tragically, while he was gone, his estate was set upon by fangbears and his young wife and child were killed. Mad with grief, he swore on his soul that he would someday have revenge upon Daffyd's house."

Keven nodded. "That tale was old even in my youth. What isn't as well remembered is that, when the dragon-lord Druin came to this land, the knight found a new master. I know not what spells the evil wizard cast over the knight, what powers were gifted, or what vengeful promises were made, but the two fought together against Valles and the White Wizard. Many thought the knight fell when his master was defeated, but, as you now know, the Dark Knight of Cumbria lives on. I fear he acts as the eyes and ears and sword of his captive master."

Rhyan shivered, remembering the cold mind-touch of the dark-armored knight. *You are one of us, golden-eyed dragon-child.*

"It is Druin that forces us on this journey." Rhyan told Keven of Elspeth's kidnapping and their quest for the talisman as they shared a breakfast of fresh bread, soft yellow cheese, and mugs of spring water.

Soon they were ready to depart.

"Remember all that Man Lyr has told you of the Faerie, my young friends," Keven cautioned, standing at the door of his cottage. "Although no true evil can touch you under the canopy of the Old Forest, be wary! The ancient and powerful magic of this place is unpredictable and dangerous. Harm no living thing under the eaves of those waking trees—plant or animal. Guard yourselves in all dealings with the Faerie. Mind that their high words do not lead you to make promises you cannot keep. Few part company with the fair ones unchanged."

"Thank you, Keven." Rhyan placed a hand on his arm. "We can never repay your kindness. Without you, the wolves would surely have caught us."

At the mention of wolves, Hale scowled and stalked away toward the forest. Collen followed, leading Beck.

"Keep a watch on your young cousin, my lady." Keven lowered his voice. "Those wolves were from the Windover kennels, I've no doubt."

I knew it! Rhyan's hand went to Man Lyr's knife in her belt.

"I do not say that Hale Plendraig would plot to betray you." Keven shook his head, and a frown drew his eyebrows together. "Only that I fear his present loyalty may be unclear to his own heart." He laid his hand on Rhyan's shoulder. "Keep thee well, lady. I think that we may meet again."

"Keep well, Keven."

Taking a deep breath, Rhyan strode under the eaves of the Old Forest.

The air hung thick and heavy with memory. Words murmured in the leaves, and branches stirred far above. Hidden eyes watched. Waited. Measured her...

I am worthy! Tell me I am worthy.

But the ancient guardians did not answer.

Hale and Collen waited a few steps down the worn pathway, their attention fixed on something hidden from Rhyan's view.

"What is it?"

"A wicked enchantment—or perhaps some trick of Keven's," Hale said.

"I think it's a Faerie-person, my lady." Collen pointed at a cluster of white trillium growing alongside the path.

The center of one of the milky flowers glowed. As Rhyan watched, the light dimmed, revealing the outline of a tiny human-like form. She leaned forward to take a closer look.

The light flared. "Stay back. Back. Back!" a high, shrill voice screeched. It echoed throughout the forest, accompanied by a choir of tiny bells.

Rhyan stepped back.

"Stay put, mortals," the voice commanded. "Stay until I pass my judgment!"

"Judgment!" Hale spluttered.

"Hush!" Rhyan remembered Man Lyr's advice and Keven's words of caution. She addressed the tiny being with respect. "Kind warden of this pathway, I apologize for the intrusion. We were merely curious—"

"Ignorant!" the voice shrilled.

"Ignorant." Rhyan agreed before Hale could start up again. "We will submit to your benevolent judgment."

The tiny being softened its glow. Rhyan could now see delicate, nearly transparent wings and whirling, silverish eyes.

"Very well," the voice piped in a kinder tone. "Answer my questions, if you please. What is your purpose here?"

"We seek the Faerie people."

"To what end?"

"Our wise friend, Man Lyr, has sent us—"

"Man Lyr!" The voice trilled, and the invisible bells clanged. "Since when have the Faerie folk listened to the sendings of a fallen one? Be gone! Be gone! Leave now, or I will curse you and your cohorts to circling this forest for the next hundred years!"

"But I have come to see the forest guardian," Rhyan interrupted. "I seek a talisman."

"Intruder! Fairie enemy!" The being's light flickered, and its tiny head turned from side to side. The bells jangled off-key.

Gooseflesh rose on Rhyan's arms. A soft, cool, sweet-smelling breeze flowed around her, displacing the heavy breath of the forest.

"Be gone! Be gone!" The glowing creature rang its bells once more and then disappeared.

As the jarring chimes faded, a dozen riders melted out of the forest and appeared on the path but a handful of paces from where Rhyan stood. Their smooth brown skin and dark hair matched the shadowed tones of the rough tree bark. The riders wore close-fitting garments colored in varying shades of green and gray. Their mounts had no saddles, halters, or reins.

"Greetings, Little Dragon. You and your fellow travelers are well come." A tall rider dressed in silver-gray moved his horse toward her. His thin, dark face bore delicate and sharp features. Rhyan's gaze followed the sculpted line of his jaw before drifting upward to meet a sea-green regard—a startling contrast to his burnished umber skin.

"Forgive us, my lord." She bowed low. Surely he heard the loud pounding of her heart. "We are grateful for your welcome but were startled by your appearance and confused by the questioning of your...um...path warden."

"Path warden?" The Faerie sniffed the air. He looked down at the patch of trillium. "Ahhh. An apology is due you, Little Dragon. My party of welcome set out as soon as we felt your presence beneath the branches of our forest, but it seems we were not in time to prevent the mischief of our small brother."

"Small brother?" Rhyan asked.

The Faerie nodded. "Yes. A pixie, I think you would call him. But there is little time for explanations. I am Ailem Suir, called First Son, and I will guide you to *Eadarowan,* the Tree City. It is the wish of the Eldest that you be brought to her with all haste."

"Fine for you to speak of hurrying," Hale interrupted. "In case you haven't noticed, we're on foot. Do you expect us to run along behind you like peasants?"

Rhyan itched to slap him.

The entire company of Faerie began to murmur in their own language.

Ailem Suir held up his hand.

"Your companion returns our greeting with hasty words." He addressed Rhyan.

"My apologies for his poor manners, First Son. My kinsman's charmed life has not readied him for the rough traveling we have encountered on our journey thus far. His temper has grown short."

The Faerie lord raised one thin eyebrow. "Your kinsman, Little Dragon?"

"Yes, my lord."

"*Ar ais agus réidh a dhéanamh*," he called out.

Three riders came forward. They dismounted and faded into the forest without a word.

"They go to tell others of your arrival and make final preparations," the First Son told Rhyan. "We Faerie prefer to travel the forest on foot and only asked the Windhooves to bear us to honor you." He waved a hand toward the horses. "These three are Firemane, Starlight, and Surefoot. They have consented to carry you to *Eadarowan*."

He turned toward Hale. "Here, Young Master, is Firemane, who will bear you. We wish all who enter our city to be honored as befits their rank. As the kinsman of the Little Dragon, we will offer you rest in *Eadarowan* and hope that we may have fair speech with you once you are recovered."

Hale's face flushed, and Rhyan stifled a chuckle. Firemane, a strong brown stallion with a reddish mane, pawed the ground and nickered. Could it be the creature was laughing at her cousin?

"Starlight will bear you, Little Dragon. He is much-loved for his sweetness and skill and, as you might guess, named for his beautiful silver coat and the dark gray marking on his wise forehead. Steady Surefoot is ready to carry your other companion."

Starlight knelt to allow Rhyan an easy mount.

"Thank you, Starlight." Rhyan clutched the stallion's mane and squeezed her thighs to maintain her balance on the horse's bare back.

"Do not fear, Little Dragon." The First Son walked his mount to Rhyan's side. "Although they will wear no saddle nor suffer other human tools, Windhooves never let their riders fall."

Starlight stood with fluid gracefulness.

Collen mounted Surefoot. He held Beck's lead in his left hand and Surefoot stretched to nuzzle the pony's head.

Mumbling under his breath, Hale scrambled onto Firemane's back.

"You have trained these horses well, First Son," Rhyan said.

"Horses? Do not demean these fair ones with such a name!" Ailem's back stiffened. He gave a quick hand signal and the party set off down the path, two by two, deeper into the forest.

"Forgive my ignorance, sir." Rhyan apologized...again.

After a moment of hesitation, the First Son nodded. "I forgive you because you have never met their kind. These are not the ponies or warhorses of a castle stable. They are of a separate race—pure and ancient—descended from Windrunner and Silverhoof, the great Windhooves brought to this land in ancient times by a long-forgotten people." He caressed the black and cinnamon mane of his mount. "Duskmane is my companion, not my servant."

"Thank you for helping me to better understand, First Son. I hope that I grow to deserve the honor I have been given by Starlight today."

"A gracious apology, Little Dragon."

Rhyan dared a look toward him and her breath caught as their eyes met. Her heart repeated its nervous thumping.

"May I ask a question?"

"You may, of course. To honor a guest, I am bound to answer, if I can."

Rhyan swallowed. "Why do you call me 'Little Dragon'?"

"Is that not your name?"

"I am named Rhyannon Kember. My friend, Man Lyr, has called me Little Dragon on occasion, but it is my kinsman, Hale of Windover who rightly bears the name Plendraig—child of the dragon. I think, perhaps, that his rudeness to you was due to your addressing me as you did."

"The Eldest bid me greet you as Little Dragon. What then shall I name you?"

"Please just call me Rhyan."

Duskmane and Starlight stopped walking as the First Son regarded Rhyan intently. "You would permit me to name you in such a way? How is it that I have earned this privilege?"

Rhyan bit her bottom lip. She remembered Keven's advice: *Mind that their high words do not lead you to make promises you cannot keep.*

"You have been courteous to us—to strangers. I feel as if I can trust you and would be honored to be your friend."

"I too have this feeling," the First Son said. "It is not something that the Faerie encounter often in someone of another race. It moves me to offer you a like gift."

He extended his hand, palm up, to Rhyan and raised his voice so that the rest of the party could hear his words.

"Rhyannon Kember, I name you as Soulfriend and I give you the right to name me *Ailem*, my mother-given name. Let all be witness to my gift."

Every Faerie in the greeting party watched and waited.

Do not insult them, Man Lyr had said.

Rhyan reached out and placed her hand over the Faerie's. Now he would surely know how her heart raced.

"Ailem Suir, First Son, I name you...Soulfriend and give you the right to name me *Rhyannon*, my mother-given name. Let all witness my giving."

"*Chéile, fírinne an fhinné!*" the Faerie responded in one voice.

Rhyan tried to ignore Hale's sullen glare and Collen's wide brown eyes, fixed on her hand resting on that of the Faerie Lord.

Her cheeks flushed, but she did not pull her hand away.

"What does it mean...Ailem?"

"*Chéile, fírinne an fhinné?* In the Common Tongue it means 'As one, we witness truth.'"

He held her hand a few seconds longer, then the moment passed. Starlight and Duskmane resumed their slow walk.

"My mind bursts with questions, Rhyannon. But I am not permitted to ask them before the Eldest has spoken with you concerning your quest," Ailem said. "In honesty, I was given permission only to answer your questions about the forest and our city-home. Mayhap I will feel the sternness of the Eldest's reprimand for this giving and receiving of names."

"I don't understand..."

"Are not names of special value to your people, Rhyannon?" Ailem asked. When Rhyan shook her head, he frowned. "More proof of my improper haste. For the Faerie people, names hold a powerful kind of magic. To give someone the use of your name is to honor them, and to give them a certain power over you. It is not a gift to be given lightly. I should apologize for asking for the exchange of names before assuring myself of your like wish."

"Please, Ailem. Now that I do understand, I am honored to share this gift with you. I have no regrets. Only, could you please just call me Rhyan?"

Ailem nodded. "That I will, Rhyan." He pointed ahead, his green eyes bright. "We approach the Gateway, my friend. Soon I will show you the wonders of *Eadarowan.*"

Rhyan peered forward. In the distance, down a corridor of mature cedars, two strangely leafless trees stood about twenty-five strides apart. The branches of each tree reached toward the other, twisting and twining into an intricate design.

"Each individual who stands before the *Wyrchide* Gate of *Eadarowan* sees something different. What you see is a glimpse of your future or a reflection of your past," Ailem explained.

Rhyan stared at the gate. *A flower? A face? An animal!*

"It's a lion." They drew to a stop before the tangled gateway. "A lion with a strange horn in the center of its head."

Ailem raised thin, dark eyebrows. He opened his mouth as if to speak, then closed it. A muscle twitched as he clenched his jaw.

The *Wyrchide* Gate swung open.

Rhyan took a deep breath as Starlight stepped across the threshold of the Faerie city. The air smelled fresher and tasted different...honeyed and sweet, but tangy, too.

It's like I can taste green and purple—like the castle garden when the first spring lilacs bloom.

Starlight nickered.

"What do you smell, friend?" Rhyan whispered. She stroked the Windhoove's neck.

'*A meadow of new hay.*' A warm, furry voice spoke in her head.

She held a hand to her brow. *Am I feverish?*

'*No. It is I, Starlight.*'

Rhyan glanced at Ailem. Had he heard the voice?

'*None of the other riders can hear my voice and none of the other Windhooves can hear your thoughts.*'

Could it really be? Starlight?

'*Yes, it is I, friend. We are mind-matched, you and I.*'

"This is amazing!" Rhyan spoke aloud.

"Yes," Ailem nodded. "I feel the same each time I return to *Eadarowan*, Rhyan. Come, the Eldest awaits."

TEN

The Tree City

As the company dismounted, a rope ladder dropped out of the leaves overhead. Two of the Faerie riders secured it to the ground and a woman descended. As dark-haired and reed-thin as Ailem, she also had the same burnished brown complexion and bright green eyes.

"Hail, daughter of Sellé," Ailem said. "I did not expect your welcome immediately upon our return. Give greeting to our guest, Rhyannon Kember, named Little Dragon by the Eldest. I have named her Soulfriend." He raised his hand and sketched a sign in the air using a strange, sinuous motion.

The Faerie woman stiffened, but bowed toward Rhyan, her face expressionless. "Greetings, Little Dragon. I am Linné, called Second Daughter. The Eldest has sent me to welcome you to our city and to give you rest and refreshment before she speaks with you."

"Thank you, Second Daughter." Rhyan returned the bow.

"I will also accompany you," Ailem said. "I would show you more of my fair home."

"The Eldest will see *you* immediately, son of Suir." A chill of rebuke coated Linné's words.

The two locked gazes, unspeaking.

"What of my fellow visitors, Second Daughter?" Rhyan asked.

Linné bowed again, but less deeply, toward Collen and Hale. "They will of course receive attention to their needs." She signaled the two Faerie flanking the ladder.

Brown eyes twinkling with eager excitement, Collen nodded to Rhyan and followed his guide nimbly up into the leaves.

Hale's ascent could not be called nimble. He clung too hard to the rope and repeatedly lost his balance. Rhyan rolled her eyes as he threw off the helping hands of his guide. Finally, he began a slow, awkward climb upward.

Rhyan turned toward the First Son. "Will I see you again, Ailem?"

He nodded with his tight, unreadable smile. "Of course."

'*As will I.*' Starlight's word's echoed in her head. '*And we will care for the little one.*'

Rhyan smiled as Beck followed Starlight from the clearing.

"Please, Little Dragon, we should make haste," Linné said.

Rhyan stepped on the ladder and put her hand on the rung above her head. The rope material felt cool and slippery—almost alive and moving against her palm. She tightened her grip.

No wonder Hale had trouble.

She climbed upward, conscious of the Second Daughter following close behind.

A circle of light became visible in the ceiling of leaves. As Rhyan drew closer, slender arms reached down through the opening and strong hands took hold of her. She fought a surge of panic when her boots lost contact with the ladder.

Bright light dazzled her eyes. The hands released their grip and she found herself standing on soft, firm ground.

"*A bheith imithe!* Begone, tiny one!" A voice commanded. The intense light vanished.

As her eyes adjusted, Rhyan discerned Linné standing before her. A tiny figure wreathed in a brilliant white aura buzzed around the Faerie's head.

"Your pardon, Little Dragon, the small brother is curious beyond the bounds of courtesy."

Rhyan looked around in wonder. Clusters of blossoming vines tumbled down from above. Large, star-shaped flowers of deep blue, purple, and gold almost covered the rich greenness of the vines. A bright ceiling soared over their heads—a living mosaic of color, luminous with captured sunlight that contrasted with the green-black, mossy floor.

"Come," Linné motioned for Rhyan to follow and set off across the space.

Soon they reached a place without hanging vines. Here, large circular tangles of whitewood branches grew up from the floor. Masses of the pale brush towered over Rhyan, taller than the autumn haystacks in Kember. Unlike the *Wyrchide* Gate, these whitewood branches bore wide, feather-like leaves and blankets of tiny blossoms in a rainbow of colors. As they passed a branch with a large cluster of bright yellow flowers, Rhyan couldn't resist...she reached out to touch one.

"Oh!" She exclaimed as the 'flower' flew away.

Linné glanced back. "The *alamathra* cannot suffer a human's touch. Your people name them butterflies."

Butterflies? Rhyan peered closer. She could just make out the almost-translucent bodies and antennas of the tiny insects, barely visible on the whitewood branches. *There must be hundreds of thousands of them.*

Ahead, Linné stopped and laid her hand on a thick branch protruding from one of the trees.

"This is your *piolin*," she said. The feather-leaves parted and formed an archway. Linné stepped inside.

Magic!

Rhyan followed the Faerie into a circular room. The *piolin* contained three distinct living areas. A wood table and two chairs formed of living hedge filled the space on her right. Against the wall at the farthest point from the entrance, a bed nestled beneath moss-colored fabric. On her left, the smooth curve of a bathing tub made of the same leafless white wood as the *Wyrchide* Gate peeked from within a tangle of concealing vines. Steam rose from the water that filled the tub and a nearby table held an array of combs, soaps, and washing cloths.

"It's lovely," Rhyan said. "Thank you."

"Your fellow travelers have been assigned their own piolin," Linné told her. "After you have spoken to the Eldest, I will guide you to their private places and you may speak with them if they desire it.

"For now, please refresh yourself in the bath. Towels and clean garments are provided. I will take your clothing to be laundered and will return shortly with your meal."

"Thank you, again, Second Daughter." Rhyan scanned the room for somewhere to undress in private.

Linné waited, staring.

Rhyan blushed.

The Faerie woman's thin eyebrows drew together. Then, her lips pressed into a slight semblance of a smile.

"Your pardon, Little Dragon. I forgot the Eldest's teachings on the customs of humans. I will turn my back as you disrobe."

Rhyan quickly removed her garments and placed them on the table before climbing into the bathing tub.

Linné turned back and picked up the dirty clothing. "If you require anything in the interim, I have posted Fiona, called Wyddandaughter, outside your *piolin*. She is well-versed in the ways of your kind."

Once the Faerie left, Rhyan picked up a bar of chunky brown-green soap. It smelled like licorice and pine needles. She ducked beneath the water, wetting her head, and worked the soap into a lather, scrubbing it into her scalp. After rinsing her hair, she used one of the soft cloths to wash her entire body. The soap stung in her minor scrapes and cuts, but after yesterday's hurried escape, the panicked run to Heart's Crossing, and a night spent on the dusty floor of Keven's cabin, it felt good to be clean.

She closed her eyes and leaned her head back against the rim of the tub. What a change from her life at Caer Kember! The Faerie treated her with profound respect and obviously recognized her importance. The face of Ailem Suir rose in her mind. His green eyes as warm as the touch of his brown hand.

A splash startled her as the bar of soap slipped from the edge of the tub. The water had grown cold while she daydreamed. Reluctantly, she climbed out and toweled herself dry.

The strange earth-brown fabric of the Faerie garments lay smooth and almost weightless against her skin. Unlike the corset and thick underclothes that she and Elspeth had been forced to begin wearing last year, the front laces and woven belt did not compress and irritate.

Elspeth. Rhyan's heart contracted as she remembered the true reason she was here among the Fairie.

Sighing, she chose a comb with widely set teeth and tried to tame her wild curls. A mirror on a shelf near the bed revealed what a futile exercise *that* was. She couldn't appear before a wise one of the Faeries with her hair in such a mess.

She went to the interior wall of the *piolin* where the doorway had been. A tentative touch of her finger opened it.

"May I be of service?" A woman moved into view. Much shorter than Linné, her round face and softer features appeared more human than Faerie. And, unlike the loose hair and decorative braids of the other Faerie women, she wore her hair in a single long braid over one shoulder.

What was her name?

"W-wyddandaughter." Rhyan's tongue stumbled over the strange title. "I was wondering…" She touched her tangled curls. "It might be unseemly to appear before the Eldest in this manner. But I am unaccustomed to dressing my own hair." She choked on the final word as she remembered Elspeth complimenting her on that last night.

Fiona Wyddandaughter put her hand on Rhyan's arm.

"Do not worry, Little Dragon." Her voice, so unexpectedly gentle. "I am here to aid you."

From a cupboard hidden in the wall of the *piolin*, the Faerie woman produced a box of hairpins, some pearled netting, and a selection of ribbon. With deft hands, she brushed out Rhyan's hair, braided it with a dark green ribbon, and twisted it into a bun. This she covered with the netting and secured in place with pins.

Rhyan sighed as she looked in the mirror. The reddish highlights in her hair shone bright against the pearls, and the neat styling made her appear older and more confident.

Ready.

"Thank you, Wyddandaughter."

The Faerie woman smiled. "You may call me Fiona."

Holding out her hand, Rhyan tried to recall the wording of the exchange of names she had made with Ailem.

Fiona Wyddandaughter shook her head.

"It is not necessary for us to use such formalities. I am not of the same–"

A whistling sound like the call of a bird echoed through the *piolin*. Fiona Wyddandaughter's smile disappeared and her eyes narrowed. "It is the Second Daughter of Faerie, asking entrance to your *piolin*." The warmth left her voice, rendering it devoid of emotion. "Do you grant it?"

"Yes." *Why the sudden change in demeanor?*

Fiona walked briskly to the doorway. She bowed to Linné and then exited the *piolin*.

The Second Daughter entered. She carried a silver tray filled with fruit and slices of a fine white bread, along with a delicate wooden goblet.

"I trust that Fiona Wyddandaughter has seen to your needs satisfactorily? She was not too familiar?"

"No. I mean, yes, thank you, she was very helpful."

"Excellent." Linné set the tray on the table. "I have brought you something to drink, Little Dragon."

Rhyan peered into the goblet. It held a deep, purplish liquid. A fruity, plum-like smell tickled her nose.

"That is *galaen*." Linné answered the unspoken question. "It is a Faerie-drink made from ripe *torthaílaen* berries. It is sweet, but not overly so. I hope you will find it thirst-quenching. Of course, I have no wish to presume. If water would be more to your liking, you have only to ask."

"Oh no, thank you." Rhyan did not want to offer offense of any kind. "I'm sure this will be fine, Second Daughter."

Very fine indeed. The sweet tangy liquid tasted unlike anything Rhyan had ever consumed. As she finished chewing the last bite of bread, she considered asking for another glass of *galaen*. Would it be impolite to do so?

A soft chiming sounded overhead. "It is time for me to take you to the Glade," Linné said. "All is ready."

Rhyan stood and the world tilted sideways. She caught herself on the table. "But my clothing..."

"Is most appropriate." The Faerie woman took her arm and led her through the door of the *piolin*.

Rhyan opened her mouth to speak but found she couldn't make a sound. She tried to stop walking, but her legs continued forward as if they belonged to someone else. In a mist of half-consciousness, she followed Linné. They came to the edge of the *piolin* grove and descended the steps of a living staircase of twining whitewood branches.

"We are leaving *Eadarowan* and entering the Sacred Glade of the Kirrin," Linné said.

A sea of strange faces floated around Rhyan. Then a pair of familiar brown eyes.

Collen?

The face disappeared behind a cloud of fog. Mist rolled and billowed in front of her eyes. She heard voices, and someone pulled on her arm. They wanted her to keep going down. Again, her legs moved without her conscious permission.

How many steps? She could see only a few feet ahead. Suddenly, she reached the bottom.

She stood alone.

A flash! Something approached through the mist.

Again! A light danced in the distance. At the back of her mind a sinuous, unfamiliar voice told her to run. *Run!* But she could not. The thick fog held her. Her feet remained weighted to the ground.

'*Do not be afraid, friend.*' Starlight's voice echoed, as if from the other end of a long tunnel. '*He will not harm you. Stand fast!*'

The bright light caught her eye once more. This time it did not disappear, but grew into a larger, shimmering, solid figure.

'*I am Gwyndarrian, the Kirrin. I am here to help you...and to test you.*'

Rhyan focused her eyes and caught her breath in recognition—the beast from *Eadarowan*'s *Wyrchide* Gate! Muscles rippled along a strong horse's body. A lion's mane flowed around the huge head as if blown by an imaginary wind. The Kirrin dipped its sharp, white crystalline horn in greeting.

Rhyan took a step toward the beast. She wanted to stroke his mane and climb on his back and ride and ride far away from Valles and this quest and...

This must be a dream.

'*In a way, you are dreaming,*' the Kirrin said. '*The Children of the Rowan have given you a drink that enables you to see me in my true form.*'

I don't understand.

'*Lay your hand upon my forehead, child. You must endure the test before we can speak further.*'

The Kirrin bowed its head and Rhyan reached out her hand. As she touched the silken brow, she felt a searching inside, as if a lantern shone into the dark corners of her heart and revealed all her secrets. Power, magic, laughter, love, pain, sorrow, triumph, escape—each flashed upon her consciousness like lightning strikes in a storm.

Then, just as suddenly, it ended. A wave of tenderness blanketed Rhyan in soothing calmness.

'At last! It is you, my Chosen. Listen well, for my time is short and I have not the power that once I knew. The forests of this world have been decimated and the Goddess forgotten by the peoples who remain. Only a few places of protection are left, and I fear that they, too, are in danger. I feel the old evil standing on the threshold of our land. Druin has returned, and with him, the corruption of nature and the murder of the innocent.'

The Kirrin bowed its head and touched the earth with its horn. A vision spread out across the patch of dirt.

The sky filled with black, billowing smoke. Children, naked and chained, marched across a burned and savaged landscape. Bodies littered the ground. Beasts rooted among the dead, and dark-clad warriors laughed as they marched on and on and on.

Bile rose in Rhyan's throat. *No, no!*

The Kirrin lifted his horn and the vision disappeared. *'I, too, despaired at this future. I cried out to the stars and pleaded with the sun—what could be done? But then, in a dream, my son Silverhoof visited me from the Shadowlands. He told me that the time had come to find the duonin—the one who is both dark and light, the one who is cursed and gifted. Then Silverhoof restored the Eyestone to me and reminded me of the Goddess's prophecy that I now give to you, duonin-Chosen.*

Star Rider must gaze into Bridelyn's Mirror
At midnight by moonrise pay heed to the seer.
Visions false, visions true
Each cannot the past undo.
River of death, secrets told
All paths lead to innocence sold.
Three swords clash—two silver, one black.
Choices made, no turning back.

Seven circles under stone
Dragon-child stands alone
In the Labyrinth's prismed eye
Seven tests to do or die
Seven faces
Seven hues
Dark future she may yet undo,
But heavy is the price of truth.'

The cold mist thickened. Rhyan shivered.

The Kirrin stepped closer and lowered his head again. This time, a silver chain slid down his glassy horn. Rhyan caught it as it fell.

A pendant hung from the chain—a milky moonstone in the shape of an eye. The iris shimmered with an opalescent light and the pupil glowed pure white.

'Use the Eyestone well. It can be a weapon of power for a duonin *dragon-child of great heart. The light and the dark must balance. Walk the prismed circuits of the Goddess. Find the center. Find your truth.'*

Rhyan slid the pendant around her neck. The Eyestone weighed cold against her skin.

'Be patient, child. You are a youngling—full of pride and desire and latent shadow. Wisdom comes with time...and sorrow. Truth is the only power.' The Kirrin dug at the ground with his hoof. *'I leave a mark to show the Children of the Rowan that you are my Chosen. Tell the Eldest of the prophecy. She will set your steps on the proper path.*

'Do not think too harshly of the prideful Faerie. Whether good triumphs or evil wins all—their world—my world—slips slowly into the twilight. It is a hard burden...'

Suddenly, the mist brightened. The Kirrin started and reared, twisting as if pain wracked his body.

'I have stayed too long, Chosen. Find the center. Find the truth.'

The Kirrin keened. Rhyan covered her ears against the piercing, sorrowful sound. Tears streamed down her face as the beast faded from sight. Soon nothing but a smattering of stars marked where his horn had been. When the mournful lament stopped, those too faded.

Rhyan shook her head to clear the last of the dream. She stood alone in the center of an arena ringed by a thick wall of evergreens.

Hundreds of eyes stared down at her.

ELEVEN

Chosen

A hand touched Rhyan's arm.

"Little Dragon, I must take you to the Eldest," Linné said.

What happened? Rhyan asked, but the Faerie ignored her. *What happened?*

'*She cannot hear you.*' Starlight's voice spoke into her confusion. '*You are still speaking only with your mind. I am in Windhoove Glade with my friends, but I have been listening for you.*'

"No." Ailem's voice suddenly echoed in Rhyan's still-clouded mind. "She has been proven. I will take her myself." He took her hand and pulled her away from Linné.

What happened, Starlight?

'*You have passed the Kirrin's Test. Now all will know who you are. For long years the Faerie have looked to their own, but it was not to be. We Windhooves knew before, but they must have their proof.*'

Rhyan put her hand to her forehead. *I don't understand...I feel as if I'm walking through cobwebs.*

'*It is the* galaen. *Breathe deep and it will pass,*' Starlight said.

What will happen now?

'Sianne of the Faerie is wondrous wise. She will help you.'

Ailem guided Rhyan through a door.

This *piolin* was much more spacious than Rhyan's. Vine curtains hinted at multiple living spaces beyond the open central room where a wide circle of empty chairs stood.

Empty—save one.

The Faerie woman stood in a slow, fluid motion. Her silver hair hung straight and unadorned, so long it brushed the hem of her forest green gown. She watched Rhyan with wide eyes that shone like liquid emeralds in her deeply lined brown face. A familiar proud white falcon perched on the back of her chair.

"My apologies, Rhyannon Kember, Bearer of the Eyestone, Chosen of the Kirrin. Our usual courtesies had to be set aside to carry out your testing, but now I give you greeting and welcome you properly to *Eadarowan*. I am Sianne, Eldest of the Faerie."

"You tricked me." Rhyan started, surprised when her words were spoken aloud. Ailem's grip tightened on her arm.

"Rhyan," he cautioned, his voice a murmur.

The Eldest waved away his concern. "Let her be, Ailem, son of my son. She speaks truth." Delicate brown fingers motioned to the empty seats. "Come, sit with me."

Linné entered the Eldest's *piolin*. She bowed to Rhyan. "Let me congratulate you on passing the Glade Test. None of your kind has ever done so."

"And if I had failed?"

"If you survived your failure, you would have woken at the entrance to our forest with no memory of your testing."

"You mean I could have died?"

"Yet you did not, Little Dragon," the Eldest said. "Kara Falcon arrived here this sunset past. She told us of Man Lyr's wish that you be given the Glade Test."

"Man Lyr mentioned no such testing to me."

What else hasn't he told me?

A hiss escaped Linné's lips. "You dare question the Eldest?"

"Enough, daughter of my daughter." Lady Sianne held up a warning hand. "You do not honor our house with this attitude."

Linné bowed her head and her grandmother continued.

"Man Lyr did indeed request that you undergo the Test and I agreed with him. The *galaen* is a necessary component to the ritual. It allows the tested to cross the bridge to the Kirrin's twilight world. I apologize for our deception, but we had to be sure."

"And are you sure now?"

"Yes. The Kirrin has left his mark in the Glade and has given you the Eyestone. You *are* the Chosen. It is only through you that we have a chance of saving our world from ruinous destruction. The evil of Druin Canwyr is breaking free and the old enchantment will not hold. The ancient and the new must be remade in some way—"

"But what of my sister?" Rhyan broke in. "My uncle, Prince Evnis, kidnapped her and took her to Windover. She holds the *Dragon's Gift*—she can renew the enchantment."

"Your sister alone is not sufficient to this task," the Eldest said. "Somehow, the *Gift* has been corrupted. This change—this weakening—has allowed Druin to grow in power and shake off the sleep that was forced upon him. It is Man Lyr's belief that, upon your birth, the magic was split. He says that you bear all the inner power, although spilling your sister's blood could have renewed the enchantment."

My power? Was I right all along? A flushing thrill of excitement gave way to a chill of deep dread. *Spilling Elspeth's actual blood?*

"What do you mean, *spilling her blood* could have renewed the enchantment? I thought the gift was some kind of magic power."

The Eldest nodded. "The enchantment was created using blood magic. Renewing it requires the spilling of a small amount of blood by the living holder of the *Dragon's Gift*. This type of magic is abhorrent to the Faerie, but it is used by wizards and others to create powerful binding spells.

"Although your sister's blood could have renewed the existing enchantment, Man Lyr fears that Prince Evnis is fully under the influence of Druin and has turned your sister over to him. The dragon-lord will use her to create a new enchantment, freeing him permanently from his labyrinth prison beneath the Tor. He will spill her blood—as much as he needs to complete the spell—and she will be powerless to resist him."

Rhyan swallowed. *Elspeth could die.*

"But if I'm the one with the strong magic, why not take me as well?"

"Evnis was blind to your power, Little Dragon. But it is plain now that Druin has discovered the error—since the Dark Knight of Cumbria pursues you."

"But my sister—"

"It is the fate of our world that should concern you!" Linné interrupted. "You are the Chosen! You hold the Eyestone! You are called to a great purpose and must not let personal feelings muddy your conviction."

Rhyan stood. "I...I ask you not to speak to me in that manner, Second Daughter of Faerie." She willed herself to remain calm. "I do care about the fate of our land. But my sister is my family and my life is my own. I will choose as I wish."

Ailem touched her arm. "Rhyan, we are not your enemies."

"Peace, Little Dragon. Ailem speaks true," the Eldest said. "There is much you will understand in time. For now, I have two questions that I hope you will answer."

Rhyan drew and released a long breath. "Of course, Eldest. I would be honored by your questions."

"Firstly, did the Kirrin speak to you?"

Rhyan closed her eyes. So much of what had passed between them she remembered only as feelings. Sadness. Warmth. Compassion. But then, in a burst of clarity, the prophecy jumped to her lips. She recited it word for word.

When she opened her eyes, the faces around her reflected

little understanding. "He said it was a prophecy from the Goddess. What does it mean?"

"The nature of every prophecy is such that they rarely provide immediate clarity, Chosen," the Eldest said. "We Faerie know, however, that words spoken by the Kirrin and fulfilled in truth will ever save us from Evil."

"But what do we do? How will we save my sister?"

"Your sister is but one small piece of this story, Chosen." The Eldest spoke with gentle firmness. "You must move beyond the selfish and think of our world, our land. The defeat of Druin is paramount. Whatever the price, he must be vanquished, or we will all face horrors unimaginable. We Faerie have long memories and can still feel the echo of blood and corruption from Druin's last war. It lingers in the soil beneath our feet."

"The Kirrin also showed me a vision where an evil army burned and murdered. It made me sick."

"Druin's work is evil and unnatural—poison to our world, my child." Lady Sianne's voice held unimaginable sorrow. "He corrupted himself when he tore the fabric of his own creation and used blood magic to become a dragon. And now that corruption bleeds into every action he takes."

"Can't the Faerie protect us?" Rhyan asked. "Don't you have magic?"

"Faerie blood offers a special affinity with green and growing things. We are also attuned to the rhythm of animal existence—the natural cycles of birth and death. We understand and honor all pure life through our roles as forest guardians. But I'm afraid we have no glamour or magic craft to combat the horrors of Druin. We are people of peace, trained as warriors only to fight those who would corrupt nature."

Rhyan closed her eyes and saw again the chained children of the Kirrin's vision. This time, Elspeth walked with them.

"What do I need to do?"

"The first line of the Prophecy gives us some direction," the Eldest said. "We know the location of Bridelyn's Mirror—the

Bridemere, as the Dalrian's call the magic lake."

"But who is the Star Rider?"

"You are, Rhyan," Ailem answered.

How many titles am I going to have? Little Dragon, Chosen, Star Rider...golden-eyed dragon-child.

"Is not Starlight your Windhoove mount?" Ailem continued. "It is clear that you must travel to the Bridemere at once."

His grandmother nodded. "But before we plan your journey, you must answer my second question, Little Dragon."

"Yes?"

"How is it that in one afternoon you have persuaded my Ailem Suir, son of my son, to name you Soulfriend and exchange the gift of mother-given names?"

"It was my idea at first," Rhyan admitted. "It felt awkward when he called me *Little Dragon.* So I asked him to call me Rhyan. Then he suggested that we 'exchange the gift,' as you put it."

"She speaks truth," Ailem said.

"Honesty becomes you, Little Dragon," the Eldest said. "I will continue to call you that name, since it is a true one. And I will not consider this breaking of our customs a transgression of honor. Nor will I reprimand you, Ailem-of-my-heart. While it is true that, among our people, approval from a parent is traditionally given before the exchange of names is performed, it is my feeling that some other force is at work here. I believe you are meant to travel the Goddess's prismed path together, for a time."

The Eldest of the Faerie closed her eyes and leaned back in her hedge chair. "I will not speak of it now. I must call a meeting of the families. Linné, see to it."

"Yes, Eldest."

"Leave me now, all of you," she whispered.

Rhyan followed the two younger Faerie from the *piolin.* Without a word, Linné left them, disappearing in the maze of colorful bushes.

"The Second Daughter doesn't like me," Rhyan said.

"Although the Faerie do not use this word, *like*, I understand your meaning," Ailem said. "She disapproves of your presence in our city and my gift of name confuses and angers her. However, the greatest obstacle to her *liking* you is that you have been named Chosen by the Kirrin. For long years she has nurtured in her heart the dream of being the savior of our people."

"I didn't ask for all of this."

"That is the single fact that wounds Linné most deeply. She who wanted it so badly was passed over in favor of one who has no desire for the honor."

But I did want it. I wanted power. Now the Eldest says that I have it in my blood. And the Kirrin has given me this talisman.

She closed her hand around the Eyestone, the edges of the pendant cutting into her palm.

Ailem brought her to the *piolin* assigned to Collen and Hale. The two sat at a small table sharing a meal. Both wore earth-brown Faerie garb.

"My lady!" Collen got up and reached for her hand.

"I'm all right."

"Thank the Crown! I should have stayed with you. I promised to keep you safe." He clasped her fingers briefly and then hung his head.

"You committed no fault, Collen William's son," Ailem said. "It was required that Rhyan Kember face the Kirrin alone."

Hale stood and cleared his throat. "I'm glad to see you are well, cousin. We were allowed in the Glade but saw nothing but bright flashes of light. What happened to you?"

Surprised by his concern, Rhyan recounted the Glade test. "The Kirrin gave me the Eyestone and a prophecy. Now the Faerie are calling me the Chosen and telling me that I have to—"

"You! Why is it always you?" Hale sputtered. "*I* am the heir to the Prince of Windover. I insist that I be given consideration."

She opened her mouth to challenge him and tell him what a spoiled fool he was, but then the truth dawned on her.

Hale wants exactly what I want. Recognition. Power.

"Rhyan Kember has been Chosen," Ailem said. "No one else may take her place."

Her cousin's scowl deepened as the Faerie continued.

"Whatever hidden qualities you hold, Hale of Windover, you certainly lack somewhat in manners. These tantrums may have gained you much within the walls of your castle-home, but you will find that in the real world, courtesy, honor, and valor are much prized. I see potential for these virtues in you, but you have not cultivated them.

"The Kirrin has made his choice and the future of our world is at stake. Those of us who have honor and love our land are ready to follow the decisions of the Wise. Will you be counted among us, Hale Plendraig? Will you start anew and grow to earn the respect and glory you desire?"

Hale's face flushed red. He held clenched fists at his side.

"I will go where Rhyan goes and see this through to the end." He answered in a tight voice, nodding to his cousin.

But your father is controlled by my enemy. I can never trust you.

"Very well," Ailem said. "Let us sit. The Chosen requires food and time to recover. And you should all prepare yourselves for the meeting of the families."

Rhyan took a small plate and selected some nuts, a soft white bread roll, and a few slices of apple. Ailem filled her goblet with purplish liquid, but she drew back, shaking her head.

"This is *sú torthaí*," he reassured her. "It is simply the fresh juice of *torthaílaen* berries diluted with spring water. I promise you that it holds no surprises." He poured himself a fresh goblet and took a drink.

"I'll have plain water, if you please," Rhyan said.

"What is this 'meeting of the families,' First Son?" Hale asked.

"It is a council of Faerie that meets in times of crisis. The eldest of each of our houses brings their heir to the Eldest's *piolin*."

"What will be discussed at the meeting?" Rhyan bit into a

slice of green apple, savoring the honey and ginger sweetness.

Ailem raised pencil-thin eyebrows. "Why, we must decide who will accompany you on your journey, of course."

A short time later, Rhyan, Collen, and Hale sat at a side table in the Eldest's *piolin*. In the center of the room, the eldest of each Faerie house occupied the circle of chairs. Behind each eldest stood the family's heir. Ailem and Linné both stood close behind their grandmother.

Collen whispered something in Rhyan's ear, but she could not hear him over the Faeries, who spoke loudly in their own language. At last, the Eldest rose from her chair and raised a delicate hand. The voices fell silent.

"I invite the Chosen to enter our circle," she said.

Rhyan made her way to the council floor. Her heart pounded. She felt as she had in the Glade arena, standing small and insignificant in the center of a circle of stern-eyed Faerie.

"Rhyannon Kember, Little Dragon and Chosen of the Kirrin, we are honored by your presence here."

"Th-thank you, Eldest," Rhyan stammered. "I hope you can help me to understand what is required of me."

"Are you not the Chosen of the Kirrin?" A silver-haired, gray-eyed Faerie lord addressed her. "I, Feärn of House Alder, must risk members of my house to accompany you and you say that you do not understand what is required?"

"I understand, sir, that I was chosen." Rhyan licked her lips. "But I do not understand why. I do not know what journey I must undertake and what task I must accomplish."

The heir of Alder stood straight and tall at her father's shoulder. "The Chosen is only a child." She addressed the council in a harsh, loud voice. "Has some mistake been made? Have we read the Kirrin-sign rightly? Our best warriors must be a part of this quest—that is the wisest course."

"There has been no mistake," the Eldest said. "Every elder

stopped in the Glade after the test and read the mark. The best proof of all is that the Little Dragon stands here before us bearing the Eyestone.

"However, I know that Tura, First Daughter of Alder, has spoken aloud what many of you feel in your hearts. Why has the Kirrin chosen outside of our people? What special gift has this girl that makes her worthy? I remind you what we all believe—that the Eyestone shall provide the power needed when the time is right. And before we proceed further, I ask all of you this question: Would anyone among you act contrary to the choice of the Kirrin?"

The Faerie sat still and silent.

"So we are decided. Now, according to the prophecy revealed to the Chosen, the first goal is to the North.

"Star Rider must gaze into Bridelyn's Mirror

"At midnight by moonrise pay heed to the seer.

"Since the Bridemere is within the gates of Rath Mormar, we must seek the Steward's permission to enter."

Rath Mormar? That's the fort of the Royal Steward from Keven's story...Bridelyn's lost kingdom...

"Little Dragon, Chosen of the Kirrin, will you choose some from among the heirs of our houses to be your companions?"

Rhyan swallowed. "I would be honored. Could someone please introduce me?"

"I will, Chosen." Fiona Wyddandaughter approached the circle of the council. Kara Falcon perched on her shoulder.

A few of the Faerie frowned, but they did not speak out when the Eldest nodded her approval.

Why don't they like her?

Fiona gave Rhyan the names of the first five heirs. After each naming, Rhyan bowed and extended her hand, palm up, in the traditional greeting. She shivered at the cold touch of the Faeries' fingers as, one by one, they laid their hands upon hers.

When Rhyan touched the hand of the sixth heir, Tura, First

Daughter of Alder, the Eyestone suddenly beamed with a brilliant white light!

A chorus of murmurs filled the room.

"It seems that the Eyestone has some choice in this matter." The Eldest appeared as surprised as Rhyan—and everyone else present. "Chosen, please continue around the circle."

Rhyan came to the place where Ailem stood.

Please let him be chosen.

A surge of relief flooded through her when the Eyestone flared at his touch.

None of the other heirs had any effect on the enchanted talisman.

"How can the Eyestone wish only two of our number to make the journey?" Tura of Alder said. "That will not be sufficient."

"Perhaps I should be tested again." Linné clearly wished to be among the party of travelers.

"No." The Eldest shook her head, setting her long, silver hair swaying. "Be content, Second Daughter. I do believe, however, that there are still some here who have not yet been tested. Hale Plendraig and Collen William's son, please come forward."

The Eyestone shone its white light as Rhyan touched Collen's trembling hand. He sighed in relief.

Rhyan extended her hand to Hale. His eyes met hers as the Eyestone lit yet again. Neither she nor her cousin smiled.

"And one more to be tried." The Eldest's voice rang out. "Fiona Wyddandaughter, place your hand into the Chosen's."

As the Eyestone glowed, a brief look of satisfaction appeared on Fiona's face. The members of the Faerie council murmured to each other in their own language.

Who is she?

TWELVE

Rough Crossing

"We will cross the West Briden here." Tura pointed to a location on the large map in the center of the whitewood table. "At the *Teorainn* Bridge."

Everyone leaned forward to examine the route that Tura outlined—except Rhyan. Her eyes shifted to the eastren part of Valles. She knew the landmarks surrounding Kember and the princedom of Windover. Man Lyr had encouraged her to study maps of the settlements and terrain around her home. But beyond the Old Forest to the southwest and the Tor to the north, she recognized little. Did people live among the rows of jagged hills along the westren coast? What lay beyond the snake and spear symbol in the south? This map made her feel small and ignorant. She ran her finger along the coastline and over to where the words "*I Wyddan—To the Wizards*" were penned at the map's edge. *By whose hand?* She longed to see more of the world...and to be more.

Linné entered the room. "The Eldest returns. She has rested in the top boughs of *Eadarowan* but is not refreshed. Her soul is heavy and tired, but she comes now to bid the company farewell."

Ailem motioned for everyone to gather before his grandmother's chair.

Sianne, Eldest of the Faerie, entered her *piolin* leaning hard on her attendant's arm. She made her way to her chair, then sat down heavily.

"The time has come for you to depart," she said. "I am weakened by age and worry, but I find strength in the hope I see in you, the Companions of the Kirrin's Chosen. I charge you to see this quest through until its end and stand by Rhyannon Kember as she carries the Eyestone and fulfills the prophecy." Her gaze stopped long upon each member of the company. "We do not know what sacrifices and courage will be necessary to save those who dwell in this land from the evil growing daily in the shadows beneath Windover Tor. But I ask, will you swear to be true to this quest and to the Chosen?"

"Aye!" Five voices answered as one.

"Wrawwck!" Kara Falcon called.

The Eldest nodded. "And you, Rhyannon Kember, Chosen of the Kirrin, do you also swear to follow this quest, wherever it may lead?"

"Aye."

"Remember, each journey leads to a truth. Sometimes, what we value most must be given away to find that truth. Remember too, some battles may be won by courageous words, honor, love, and inner strength—not by weapons and brute force."

"Perhaps, then, I am poorly chosen for this mission." Tura frowned and gripped the hilt of her sword. "After all, my skill is with blade, bow, and spear. I am not known for my prowess with words."

The Eldest smiled. "Rest assured, First Daughter of Alder, there will be armed conflict enough on this journey."

Sianne turned her penetrating regard back to Rhyan. "To the Chosen, I extend this reminder: Look inside. Know yourself. Be true."

Rhyan raised her chin and held the Faerie's gaze. *I carry many good qualities. I have courage. I am strong. I am wise for my years. I will conquer our enemies and rescue Elspeth. I will!*

But what do I want more? To find Elspeth? Or to wield true power and be a hero?

The Eldest closed her eyes and sighed.

No! I love Elspeth! Please, please let her be kept safe—she must stay safe until we find her.

"Farewell, Chosen. May you find your truth."

The six travelers sat astride their Windhoove mounts at the *Wyrchide* Gate. The whitewood glowed like bleached bones in the half-light of dawn. Rhyan tried to make out the face of the Kirrin that she had seen in the Gate on her way into the city, but the tangled branches revealed nothing.

Is my future empty?

Ailem touched her arm. "It is time, Rhyan."

Tura and Collen led the party, while Rhyan and Ailem followed. Hale and Fiona brought up the rear, with Kara perched on the Faerie woman's shoulder.

As they followed the forest path away from *Eadarowan*, Rhyan couldn't resist a glance back at the *Wyrchide* Gate. The sharp outline of a woman's face took shape in the twisted wood. A familiar young woman with strange eyes and a sad, wounded expression.

"What do you see?" Ailem asked.

"Nothing."

It is my own face. But what happened to me?

By midmorning the travelers had reached the northwestren edge of the Old Forest. Rhyan's nose tickled as the brown, earthy smell of the woods gave way to the warm perfume of the rolling, green-gold meadows that tumbled from the brush line down toward the distant, sparkling brightness of the River

Briden. The company halted beneath the last branching arms of the ancient trees, and Rhyan looked out on the hazy, overcast landscape.

'*It will be good to run,*' Starlight said.

"Ho there!" Tura shouted. She signaled them to stay under cover and waved toward a grassy hill that rose among the blooming wildflowers some distance away.

A tall figure in a red cloak and hat appeared from behind the knoll.

Keven?

Tura urged Darkmane, her Windhoove mount, across the meadow. Reaching the figure, she dismounted and drew her sword.

"Wait!" Rhyan shouted.

"Fear not, Chosen," said Fiona. "Tura is long acquainted with the son of Trallendon. She has no doubt pulled her weapon to berate him for wearing his red garb again. She says it makes him too easy a target for a hidden archer."

As the rest of the party crossed the meadow, Tura sheathed her sword. But the Faerie woman's angry voice carried on the wind. "All courtesy aside, I will put an arrow in you myself if you don't stop wearing that cloak!"

Keven bowed, his scarlet cape billowing out behind him in the brisk morning breeze. "Greetings to you, First Son." He lifted a hand as Ailem approached.

"Greetings, Keven of Tralleigh," the First Son said. "How is it that you are so far from Heart Crossing?"

"Bridelyn says the Dark Knight and his wolves have made their way across the delta and boggy plain on the coast. They will certainly cross the River Trall—waters Bridelyn cannot touch. I fear they mean to overtake Rhyan Kember before she reaches the *Teorainn* Bridge."

Rhyan shivered, remembering the chilling grip of the knight's magic.

With a loud cry, Kara Falcon took off from Fiona's shoulder

and circled above them.

"She will warn us if the knight or his beasts approach," Fiona said.

"Friend Keven, your warning is timely, but how did you know where to find us?" Ailem asked.

Keven looked away, toward the river. "Bridelyn told me. She knows the Kirrin sends you to the Bridemere. She set me free—released me from our vow—so that I could not only alert you of the knight's approach, but also caution you not to visit the magic lake."

"But why?" Rhyan asked. "We are not her enemies."

"Something is happening." Keven's brows drew into a troubled frown. "I feel an end approaching and Bridelyn feels it too. After all these years, she still wishes to protect her people. She is not evil, only afraid, and you are at the center of her fear, Rhyan Kember."

"And this Bridelyn is the oracle that will speak at the Bridemere?" Tura asked. "She is already against the Chosen! The Kirrin's message is indeed clouded."

Ailem shook his head. "The message was clear. We go on." He motioned toward the water rushing in the distance. "Let us make a ford of the West Briden."

"But, how?" Fiona asked. "Even should we do so safely, Bridelyn will sense our presence as soon as we touch the waters."

"True." Keven nodded. "But although she possesses the ability to drag her enemies to their deaths, I do not think she would harm us. She acts only to protect her people."

"You, too, have power over the river, Keven of Tralleigh," Hale burst in. "We saw how you moved your boat across the water at Heart Crossing without paddle or rope line."

"My 'power,' as you call it," Keven said, "is the ancient enchantment of the Crossing itself. But we are very far indeed from that place of peaceful magic." He turned toward Ailem. "Even without Bridelyn's presence, this would be a dangerous crossing, First Son. The river is swift-flowing and as cold as the mountain snow."

"The Dark Knight of Cumbria and his unnatural wolves are our alternative," Ailem said. "We must trust in our strength and in Bridelyn's mercy."

"I am not afraid to go anywhere Darkmane will carry me." Tura stroked the neck of her Windhoove mount.

'The Windhooves fear nothing.'

Starlight's brave words comforted Rhyan, but the worry in Keven of Tralleigh's eyes gave her pause.

"River of ice and enchantment, or bloodthirsty wolves." Hale looked pointedly at Rhyan. "Let us choose and take action."

Firemane tossed his head and neighed as if to agree.

Kara Falcon suddenly swooped down onto Fiona's shoulder. She ruffled her feathers and made a brief whistling sound.

"The enemy approaches!"

The howling call of a wolf echoed on the misty morning air.

"To the river!" Ailem shouted.

Tura reached down to help Keven mount behind her on Darkmane.

"Leave me." He pushed away and attempted to slide to the ground. "I do not wish to weigh you down in the river. I will fend for myself."

Tura pulled him back in place, and Darkmane tossed his head.

"He says that he will not leave you to meet the wolves and will forgive your rude assessment of his abilities," Tura said.

"Away! Away!" Collen shouted.

They raced across the meadow. The pounding of hooves echoed in Rhyan's ears, but the sound of wolves howling and barking soon grew louder.

"There!" Tura pointed to the right.

The dark silhouettes of six wolves appeared on the crest of a grassy knoll only three or four rises away.

"Run, Starlight. Run," Rhyan murmured.

'I run as fast as I am able. Fear not. The northren wolves will not

catch us before we reach the water. I will take the quickest route.'

Sure enough, the next rise of meadow fell away to reveal the River Briden flowing cold, swift, and dark.

"*Hiya! Bíodh feasacht láidir agat! Fágann an t-uisce go fuar,*" Tura called out as Darkmane entered the frigid water.

"She says the river becomes deep very quickly and is colder than she thought," Ailem shouted. "Take care!"

As the other Windhooves slowed their pace to maneuver around a tumble of large boulders, Starlight broke toward the left and cut through a trio of bushes. But two wolves appeared from the cover of the thicket. He reared and gave the Windhoove warning call.

The beasts nipped and growled, keeping well away from Starlight's slashing hooves. Rhyan fought to maintain her balance. She looked back. Three more wolves blocked their retreat.

"Up the hill!" She pointed to their immediate left.

As Starlight turned in that direction, a wolf launched itself onto his flank. Black claws gripped savagely, and the stallion roared as yellow teeth sank into his flesh.

Rhyan pulled the knife Man Lyr had given her from her belt and plunged it into the wolf's neck. Warm, black-red blood pulsed over her hands. The Eyestone tingled against her chest.

The dead wolf fell away, and Starlight surged toward the crest of the hill, blood streaming from his wound.

The skirmish surely continued around her, but Rhyan felt and heard only the thumping of her heart. Her vision narrowed.

I killed it.

The thick blood began to dry on her hands, tightening like a binding rope. As it cooled, the tingling of the Eyestone faded.

Starlight staggered slightly as he reached the edge of the cliff. Rhyan shook her head, coming back to herself as the Windhoove's muscles tensed, readying for the jump down.

'Dragon-child.'

Rhyan turned and looked back down the hill, over the heads of her companions, still struggling against the wolves. Like a blot on the sun, the Dark Knight stood motionless at the edge of the golden meadow. She remembered her vision beneath the tree in Eldon Wood.

A dark-armored hunter with black bow in hand.

He nocks a red-fletched arrow and points it toward the heart of the sleeping deer.

'You are one of us, golden-eyed dragon-child.'

Rhyan opened her mouth to yell out a denial, but no words came.

The fell knight loosed his arrow.

'We know what the Beast of the Forest has given you. Bring my master the Eyestone and you will have your sister and all that you desire.'

Rhyan watched, strangely calm, as the gleaming black arrow sped toward her. She admired the smooth shaft and the careful fletching. It rotated slowly, carving through the morning mist. Slowly, slowly... Just before the barb would have pierced her heart, the dark projectile burst into a thousand glittering fragments. The shimmering dust enveloped her. She breathed deeply.

A wave of heat raced through her veins. In a rise of breathless clarity, Rhyan saw herself soaring above a city of gleaming black stone. Thousands of people below called her name "Rhyannon! Queen Rhyannon!"

Her hands loosened their grip on Starlight's mane. She spread her arms to revel in the thrill of the flight.

"I am here! I am here, my people!"

"Rhyan!" Ailem's call echoed.

His arms tightened around her just before she spiraled into unconsciousness and they fell down, down, down into the swirling, frigid waters of the river.

THIRTEEN

Shadow Dream

Rhyan's spirit flew through dense clouds and out into the open sky. A multitude of stars winked a diamond-bright welcome. She flew on and on. Soaring and twisting, she rode the gusts and eddies of the untamed wind.

Then she felt a pull, as if someone below called out to her. She drifted downward, and far below, the outline of a flat-topped mountain came into view.

Windover Tor.

She dove through the rock and the sweet-smelling earth, passing through dirt and stone with no more effort than she had expended flying through the clouds or the starry sky.

Emptiness opened around her. A small white form lay curled and shivering in the darkness. The figure sat up and brushed away loose straggles of hair that hung about a pale, smudged face.

Elspeth.

Rhyan flew down close and tried to touch her sister, but her dream hand passed through Elspeth's fingers and brought no comfort.

Elspeth covered her bare feet with the remnants of a torn and filthy blanket. She closed her eyes and sang in a broken whisper. Rhyan recognized the old lullaby that Nanny used to croon to them at bedtime:

Sail away
To the starry sea
Where the Moon will grant your sweetest dream
And the goddess smile on thee, my child
The goddess smile on thee.

The flicker of a candle flame bounced off the damp rock walls as booted footsteps drew closer. Elspeth turned away, shielding her eyes.

"Elspeth," a voice called from the door. "Would you like to take a walk with me? Out under the stars? Afterwards, you could stay in the guest room in the castle. I've had a pretty dress made for you. You could put it on for dinner. I've ordered a scrumptious meal with lamb pie and fresh bread."

The words sounded so inviting, so friendly, so normal. Dream Rhyan hoped that Elspeth would agree and that, maybe, the world would go back to the way it had been.

"Could I wash my hair and bathe?" Elspeth's raspy voice cracked.

"Of course." The voice grew louder. "But first we must pay a visit to someone down the hall. Do you remember my friend who needs your help? You will help him, won't you?"

"Yes, Uncle." Elspeth uncovered her eyes.

"Good, good." Prince Evnis of Windover entered the cell. "Here, let me take your hand. That's a good girl. Just a few steps."

Elspeth clung to his arm as he led her down the passageway to a heavy door of dark metal.

Rhyan tried to cry out a warning to her sister, but she could make no sound.

Evnis pushed the door open and led Elspeth through. After a few paces, the narrow passageway opened into an enormous vaulted cavern. A murky red glow lit the space, except for a dark, impenetrable shadow, huddled near a strange gate in the center of the chamber.

"What have you brought me, Evnisss?"

The prince cleared his throat. "I bring the eldest of my sister's blood, holder of the *Dragon's Gift*. She has consented to help you, my lord."

"We shall sssee," the unseen speaker hissed. "Come here, child."

Elspeth swayed on her feet, clearly unable to hold herself upright. Evnis took her arm and guided her a few unsteady steps forward.

"Enter, child," the voice commanded.

Elspeth shuffled toward the gate.

As she moved closer, the shadow expanded and throbbed in the red-tinged half-light. She placed her hand on the gate, then stopped, shaking.

With snake-like stealth, the thing reached out one scaled limb.

Elspeth moaned aloud.

No! No! Rhyan screamed soundlessly.

An ebon claw touched Elspeth's neck.

Her scream echoed throughout the chamber. When the claw removed itself, she crumpled to the ground like a cloth doll.

Elspeth?

"When she rouses, return her to her cell, Evnisss. Keep her sssafe until the day of the moondark. If her sssister fails to bring me the Eyestone, I will need her blood to keep free from prison. I charge you with thisss one—since you were not wise enough to bring both to me."

A trickle of perspiration ran down Evnis's temple and into the corner of his mouth. His tongue flicked out and licked the salty sweat. "She was not firstborn, my lord. I thought her of little consequence to us. How could I know that the bearer of the *Dragon's Gift* was not also the bearer of the hidden power you required?"

"Ignorant fool! But...no matter, my dark ssservant is in pursuit of her. Ssshe will come to me and join me in my great enterprise."

"I am also your loyal servant, my lord." Evnis bowed. "Once more I crave pardon for this unfortunate mistake."

"Be at ease, Evnisss, this is turning out to be quite entertaining. I received a message from my ssservant some hours ago. It contained a note which may be of interest to you."

"And what is that, my lord?"

Although the creature's face remained cloaked in darkness, Rhyan felt the evil thing smile. "It ssseems your ssson is accompanying the girl."

Evnis betrayed no emotion. "I cannot be accountable for his actions, my lord. His blood runs too close to his mother's."

"If the girl proves an enemy, would you have him ssspared?"

"He has made his choice. Let him answer for it."

The evil thing chuckled. "You are a cold and heartlesss man, Evnisss. Perhaps that is why we work ssso well together."

Elspeth stirred on the floor. Evnis bent and lifted her into his arms.

"I will return her to the cell, my lord."

Elspeth? Rhyan hovered close to her sister's face. *I'm here! Open your eyes!*

Elspeth's eyelids flickered.

Icy hands gripped Rhyan's arms.

'Wake, Rhyannon Kember! I save you now to give you fair warning. Abandon this quest! Seek not the Bridemere! Do not endanger my people! Your desire for power will destroy many...will destroy those you love. Turn back, turn back!'

The hands pulled Rhyan away, tearing her dream-self back through the mountain, into the clouds and...

Far away from her sister.

FOURTEEN

To the Gates of Rath Mormar

Her eyes flickered open in the darkness. Pain. Unceasing, aching pain. She tried to lift her head, but sharp darts of searing agony shot across her forehead.

"Move carefully, Chosen," Fiona said.

"Where are we?" Rhyan whispered.

"Safely across the West Briden and camped on the Dalrian lowlands." Fiona touched the water bag to Rhyan's lips. "Drink."

The cool liquid soothed her parched throat.

"What happened?"

"We are not sure, exactly. The Dark Knight's arrow covered you with some foul fog. You shouted and fell from Starlight's back into the river. You've been unconscious for hours. There was also some bruising on your right hip and..." Fiona fell silent.

"What is it?" Rhyan asked.

"Your right arm was broken."

Rhyan flexed the arm. Her muscles ached, as from a deep bruise, but the limb was whole.

"Could the Eyestone be healing me?"

Fiona shifted in the darkness. "I have never heard that the Eyestone has that power. Keven agrees. He says there is something else hidden within you—something he doesn't recognize. Something that is...coming to life."

You are one of us, dragon-child.

"What of Starlight? He was...bitten. I struck the wolf with Man Lyr's knife."

"He is not in danger. The wound is long, but not deep. We have much skill in treating the injuries of the Windhooves. I myself packed the dressing with honey and some fresh *leigheas* I found growing nearby."

"Thank the Crown." Rhyan sighed—and groaned as the pain is her head flared again.

"Finish this, Chosen." Fiona held a wooden cup to her lips. "It will ease your discomfort and allow you to sleep."

"I shouldn't. We must continue. Aren't the wolves following us?"

"Bridelyn did not allow the Dark Knight and his wolves to ford the river into Dalria. They were forced to continue to *Teorainn* Bridge and will be many hours behind us."

It must have been Bridelyn who spoke to me...warned me. But how can I give up this quest?

She gazed up at the midnight sky. Familiar stars stood out against the velvet darkness, comforting her. Bilden, the constellation of the Smith, hung directly overhead and the first six bright stars of the Arrow of Trall pointed over the hills to the south. In the east, toward Kember, Llinos and Catrin, the Sisters, still held hands, together for eternity.

Elspeth.

Fiona coaxed a tiny mouthful of the draught between Rhyan's reluctant lips. "Everyone rests now. You and Starlight are not the only casualties. Collen William's son was slashed in the leg and lost much blood."

"Will he be all right?"

"Aye, the danger is past. Sleep will help. The First Son has ordered that we are to remain here until first light."

"Ailem..." Rhyan whispered, remembering his arms around her as they plunged into the river. "Where is he?"

"He watches," Fiona said. "We do not know if other enemies await us here."

"Fiona, I have wanted to ask you...why was the Second Daughter so angry about my name sharing with Ailem? And why is it permitted for me to speak your name without a formal sharing?"

Fiona averted her eyes. "Many of the Faerie were shocked that the First Son gave you his name. Only once before has a Faerie shared names with someone outside of our race. The result was a tragedy." She sighed. "The Faerie who shared her name was my mother."

"I am sorry." Rhyan reached out a hand to comfort her, but fell back, dizzy, as the sleeping draught began to take effect. "Forgive me, I—"

"Chosen, you must sleep now."

"I can't." She struggled against the drug. "My sister. I saw her."

"A dream." Fiona laid a gentle hand on her shoulder.

"No, it was real, a true dream. There was darkness and...blood. And Bridelyn, I—I think she spoke to me."

"Rest now, Chosen. Sleep without dreams. Sleep in peace."

Morning dawned, cold and dreary. Rhyan woke to the sound of the Windhooves calling to each other through the mist.

She yawned. *What are they going on about?*

'We greet Firefoot, our great brother in the sky,' Starlight's voice answered. *'Even though we are hidden from each other by these clouds, we must hail his faithful presence. How are you, my friend?'*

Rhyan smiled. *I am happy to hear you, Starlight. My head is clearing and my arm mending well—but what of your wound?*

'Fear not, friend. I have been well tended. Wait and see.'

"Rhyan, you must wake now." Ailem's voice interrupted.

She opened her eyes and struggled to sit up. "I am awake."

"Easy, my friend." He slid his arm behind her back. "Do not push yourself too soon. A broken arm is no small thing."

Rhyan tried to ignore the pulsing throb inside her head. She had a momentary sense of the world shifting beneath her and clutched at Ailem with both hands.

"Your arm! The Wyddandaughter told me it had healed, but I did not believe it. I saw the break."

"Fiona tended me well. And...she and Keven say that..." Rhyan couldn't keep the tremor from her voice. She leaned against him and breathed in his musky pine scent. He pulled her close.

"What is it, Rhyan?"

"They say that I am...healing myself with my own...*power*."

His muscles tensed against her. "This is very troubling. Such power could be an attack—a corrupt enchantment of some kind. You should rest, and I must try to seek counsel. I think–"

"I will ride," Rhyan said. "We must continue. But Ailem, I saw Bridelyn in my dream. She saved us from the river. But she does not wish us to visit the Bridemere. She warned me that the price of doing so would be terrible. She says I must turn back."

"We keep to our path." Ailem's jaw tightened. "And you are right, we should move with as much speed as possible to stay ahead of the Dark Knight and those wolves—abominations of nature! Perhaps we can speak to Keven further about Bridelyn as we travel.

"Ah! Here is your breakfast."

Collen approached, limping, his right leg bound. Hale followed, carrying a bowl of steaming liquid.

"Good morning, my lord, my lady," Collen said.

His eyes focused on Ailem's supporting arm. Rhyan blushed but didn't have the strength to shift away.

"Master Hale has brought a bit of the broth we had for our supper last eve."

"Thank you, Collen," she said as Ailem reached to take the small bowl for her. "It is good to see you up and around. And thank you too, Hale."

Her cousin wouldn't meet her eyes. "Collen was injured coming to my aid. It's the least I can do, to lend him a hand with his duties."

Rhyan opened her mouth to speak, but Collen held a quick finger to his lips. Instead, she breathed in the warm, earthy scent of the soup. "It smells delicious."

"Oh, it is good," Collen said. "The Faerie gathered a few wee plants and roots and such. I didn't think it would amount to much, but along with the biscuits and that *sú—sú—sú torthaí*, what a feast for a sorry soul it was."

"I'm sorry I missed it."

"Thank the Goddess you're here with us to have a bit this morning, my lady." Collen swallowed hard. "When I saw the wolf attack Starlight, I feared the worst."

Hale turned on his heel and walked away without a word.

"Me *and* the Lord Hale were some relieved to hear you weren't seriously hurt."

Rhyan raised an eyebrow. "No need to gloss over my cousin's extreme dislike of me, Collen."

"Oh, no, I think you've mistaken him a bit. He was sincerely concerned. But, well...it's not really my place to say all these things anyway, my lady."

Rhyan remembered Evnis's words from her dream: *He has made his choice.*

Have I truly misjudged Hale?

Soon the company resumed their journey. They traveled north, following the *Ice Abain*—a name Ailem said meant 'Stream of Sorrows'—that flowed from the Bridemere at Rath Mormar down to the West Briden.

The rocky and uneven Dalrian terrain slowed their progress. Though Starlight did his best to choose his steps with care, the constant jarring motion soon elevated the throbbing in Rhyan's head to an agonizing level. She passed the hours in silent torture.

"*Stad!*" Ailem called a halt.

A rest, at last.

They'd stopped in a hollow near a stand of tall, fragrant cedars. Mossy grass covered the ground and tiny white flowers bloomed between a tumble of boulders at the edge of the stream.

Starlight nickered. '*Chosen, strangers approach.*'

Three burly, bearded warriors emerged from the cedars. Sleeveless woolen tunics left their muscled arms and thick necks plainly visible. The hilt of a heavy sword could be seen above one shoulder of each warrior. All three men rode large, shaggy-coated horses. Rhyan had never seen any animals so tall.

'*Our northren cousins are strong indeed,*' Starlight told her. '*Their thoughts are simple, though. Two of these are still thinking of the grain they ate at sunrise and the other has a stone in his hoof.*'

Despite her pain, Rhyan smiled at the concern in Starlight's thoughts.

The largest warrior, a man with a reddish beard and an ugly scar across his left cheek, motioned for the others to halt.

"I am the Bertram, captain and *laoch cìobair* to Morgan mac-Neill, the Steward of Dalria." The redbeard's booming bass voice roared. "State your purpose here."

"We are making our way to Rath Mormar, good warriors." Ailem gave a slight bow. "It is our intention to consult the Bridemere."

"The haunted pool can mean death for some," Captain Bertram said. "Who are you, and why do you desire to gaze into that perilous water?"

"We are the Companions of the Kirrin's Chosen. A quest of foremost importance has led us to your gate," Ailem answered. "Perilous or no, we must visit the Bridemere."

"It is the Steward's word that governs here," the captain said gruffly. "It is he who will decide where travelers on Dalrian land may or may not go."

"Then I humbly ask permission to speak with him," Ailem said.

"Granted," the captain said. "We are bound to welcome to all who bow to our Steward's rule. Follow me, then. My men and I will accompany you to the fortress."

Rhyan and Starlight rode with Ailem and Duskmane. As they fell in line behind the captain, Ailem told her something more of the history of Rath Mormar.

"Rath Dalria, fort of the Winter Sun, was built as a wedding gift for the Dalrian princess, Cylene. At the peak of their power, the Dalrian mages formed the palace out of the hard, white, mountain stone without tools or workmen, and moved their people from their mountain homes into the vastness of the finished fortress.

"The people flourished. Theirs was a society where each member's talents were cultivated and valued. At the base of this structured community was magic. The noble families held the mage power. To keep their abilities strong, they did not marry outside their class.

"The lesser Dalrians, not able to depend on magic, formed clans of skilled craftsmen, fierce hunters, and brave warriors." Ailem motioned toward Captain Bertram. "They worshipped the royal family, almost as if they were gods.

"A fierce pride led all of the Dalrians to become scornful and suspicious of other races. They isolated their society from the rest of the Land."

"Yes, we are prideful." Captain Bertram turned back to ride alongside Rhyan and Ailem. "And we are mistrustful of *taobh a muigh*—outsiders, as you would call them."

"Your pardon, *laoch ciobair*," Ailem said. "I meant only to inform the Chosen of your long history before she meets the Steward."

The captain nodded. "I take no offense, First Son. I only say that our caution comes from the suffering caused by the long war with the wretched Trallendon and the death of our royals."

"Yet, did not the Trallendon pay a more terrible price?" Keven spoke up from behind them. "Their race was lost and the Dalrians continue."

"Keep silent," Tura snapped.

Captain Bertram signaled a halt. He turned and faced Tura, his stern gaze narrowing on the Faerie warrior and the red-garbed Keven of Tralleigh riding behind her.

"Our history tells of the chief traitor, the son of the Trallendon who selfishly pursued our princess and caused a war through the murder of our prince. We've heard tales that he lives on in immortal punishment, bound to the River Briden where the soul of Bridelyn is trapped. They say he is dressed in bright blood red to broadcast his perfidy to all he meets.

"If those tales be true, that last Trallendon would do well to avoid Rath Mormar."

Rhyan's eyes darted from Keven to the Dalrian captain.

He knows who Keven is.

FIFTEEN

The Court of Justice

A wall of sharp white spires surrounded the vast and beautiful fortress of Rath Mormar. The main keep covered more ground than the entire castle complex at Caer Kember. Immense doors of smooth, silver-white metal opened onto a courtyard bustling with people and animals.

As the company entered, the Dalrians stopped and stared at the visitors. Like Captain Bertram, most of the men wore beards. The tall, brawny women coiled their thick red or black hair in braids about their heads. All wore layers of plaid cloth and furs, cut generously and loose.

But the smell... Rhyan's pounding head swam with the thick, pungent scents of sweat and dung.

"The Steward is presiding over the Court of Justice in the Hall of Mirrors," the captain said. "The clan petitioning should end shortly, and he will hear your request." He motioned them forward. "We will enter the Hall here. Your beasts will be taken to the stables and tended."

"We appreciate the offer of your fine stables, *laoch cìobair,*"

Ailem said. "But I must ask that you lay no hand upon the Wind-hooves. We will bid them follow you, if you can promise that they not be touched."

Captain Bertram raised his formidable brows but did not question the First Son's request. "I so promise." He gave orders to his men.

Rhyan dismounted at Ailem's signal. Pain thrummed behind her eyes. She stumbled, off balance.

"Chosen?" Fiona Wyddandaughter reached out a firm, steadying hand.

"I'm all right." She followed Ailem as the captain led them through the doors of the Hall of Mirrors.

Silver-bright, polished metal walls lined the large hall. As she moved forward, Rhyan caught a glimpse of her own face reflected there. Her eyes glowed with an inner light, glistening like polished gold-amber. The lines of her face had sharpened. She looked older, more confident, stronger.

But I feel terrible. If only this headache would end.

As she gazed at her reflection, a jeweled crown appeared on her head and her travel-stained clothing dissolved into a shimmering golden gown. The crowd of Dalrian clanspeople behind her faded and the room instead filled with tall, pale, beautiful courtiers dressed in gem-hued robes. Most wore their long, silver hair in elaborate braids. They danced in pairs around and around the mirrored hall.

Rhyan turned from the vision and found Fiona at her side. The glittering figures from the reflection had disappeared and she once again followed Captain Bertram through the crowd.

The captain halted as he approached the Steward. Two petitioners—a man and a woman—faced away from Rhyan's party, standing ready to receive the judgment of their leader. She had a clear view of the stern figure of the Steward of Dalria. His large, muscular frame filled the smooth whitestone throne. He had a wide brow and piercing blue eyes. Auburn hair fell to his shoulders, a shade lighter than his trimmed beard. He wore a simple tunic, cut of rich blue fabric and edged with black braid. A round brooch of silver metal marked with strange runes was his only ornament.

As the Steward spoke, his deep voice carried the length of the Hall.

"Having heard both sides of this sorry tale, I find that I can make no fit judgment as to the ownership of the bull in question—called 'King' by some. Therefore, it is my word that the animal be slaughtered and the meat divided equally between the two who stand here before me."

The woman put her hands on her hips and nodded in agreement. The man hung his head.

"Do you accept this justice?" the Steward asked.

"I do!" The woman's voice rang out.

"Begging your pardon, my lord Steward," the man mumbled.

"What is it?"

"Ye can give King to her. I could not bear him to be killed. He is the best stud bull in our land, my lord, and deserves better than to be anyone's dinner."

The Steward of Dalria smiled. "Aye, good Monty, I see that you could not." He leaned toward the bailiff who waited at his elbow. "Bailiff Connor, the bull, King, is the property of Monty of clan Scott. You will fine the Widow Duncan five chickens for her dishonesty."

A ripple of laughter and hand-clapping followed the Widow Duncan as she strutted away, protesting.

Rhyan winced at the sound. But, even through her pain, she recognized the great wisdom of the Steward's judgment.

He is the kind of leader I would be. I will be. Ohhh...

The pain in her head intensified. She needed rest. She needed silence.

The Steward motioned, and the bailiff sounded a large bell. Rhyan wanted to cry out at the resonating clang, but somehow remained silent as the crowd exited the hall.

"My lord Steward." The captain approached the throne and

bowed.

"Captain Bertram, who have you found wandering our borderlands? Surely these good people cannot be responsible for the beasts that have been terrorizing our livestock?" Morgan macNeill's deep blue gaze touched upon each of his visitors.

"I think not, my lord. They claim to be on a quest of some importance. They call themselves 'Companions of the Kirrin's Chosen' and wish to look into the Bridemere."

"Hmmm." The Steward rose from his seat and stepped down from the dais.

"They seem to be *mostly* honorable folk." Captain Bertram's gaze drifted toward Keven.

"Indeed. Then I, Morgan macNeill, Steward of Dalria, give you welcome. Who is this 'Chosen'?"

"Rhyannon Kember is she whom we call Chosen, my lord." Ailem stepped forward and motioned toward Rhyan.

"Cannot the Chosen answer for herself?"

She opened her mouth to speak, but the simple act of drawing breath drained the last of her strength. Needles of pain plunged into her head in a great crushing wave. Ailem reached for her.

Then, nothing.

SIXTEEN

The Steward of Dalria

Hot, acrid air filled Rhyan's lungs. A soul-swallowing darkness surrounded her. In the distance, a flickering light appeared. As it moved closer, Rhyan's eyes adjusted and the form of a woman took shape. She wore a long, rose-red velvet gown and walked, head bowed, with exaggerated grace. Long, curling tendrils of golden hair obscured her face.

"Elspeth?" Rhyan managed the single word.

The golden-haired figure stopped a few feet away and lifted her head. Two black, shining eyes stared out. Ruby lips opened in an evil grimace, revealing sharp white fangs. Elspeth's body became a mass of red scales, bursting from her dress.

"No!" Rhyan screamed. The candle fell to the ground and went out.

"Rhyan?" A gentle voice pierced the fog of her dream.

She struggled against the arms that held her.

"Rhyan Kember, wake up!"

"Elspeth?" Rhyan pried her eyes open. She lay in a soft bed in a richly appointed but unfamiliar sleeping chamber. The smooth walls gleamed as white as new snow.

Rath Mormar.

"No, Chosen. It is Fiona Wyddandaughter."

"I'm sorry, Fiona, my sister is much on my mind. I think Man Lyr was wrong, I should have followed her to Windover."

The Faerie woman stiffened. "I have no doubt the wise Man Lyr knew the best course." She released Rhyan and turned away.

Why does she always act so strangely when I mention him?

"Are you acquainted with Man Lyr?" Rhyan asked.

"Indeed, I am." Fiona did not turn around. "And I feel it is time I told you the truth. He is—"

A brisk knock on the door of the chamber interrupted her answer.

"Enter," Fiona called. She placed her hand on the hilt of the dagger at her belt.

Ailem entered, followed by the Steward of Dalria.

"I am glad to see you feeling better, Rhyan," Ailem said.

She sat up in the bed and managed a thin smile. "Fiona has been using her magical healing powers on me again."

"True magic?" Morgan macNeill burst out. His fair face flushed red. "I beg your pardon, Rhyannon Kember, but my people little like magic of any kind. It would be wise to keep such skills secret while you are here at Rath Mormar."

"The Chosen jests, I assure you, Lord Steward," Ailem said. "But it does seem strange that your people would shy from magic, seeing they use this castle as their capital and live so close to the Bridemere."

"This castle is a marvel," Morgan admitted. "It was built with no sign of bricks and carved rock but only the smooth whiteness of mage-formed stone. Five towers and over a thousand mirrors. The gates that protect the castle are as strong as ice steel, but light enough that a mere stripling boy can turn the winch to raise them. I could go on and on about the wonders of my home. But while Rath Mormar was formed with magic, it is not magic in itself.

"Our history has made my people fear such unnatural power, First Son. We know the spirit that abides in the waters of the River Briden. We know that, on every night that the moon's light shines, that spirit makes its way up the *Ice Abain* to the Bridemere. And we know the sometime fate of those who would consult that trapped soul.

"More than three times one hundred years ago, Taran mac-Neill, Steward of Dalria, consulted the oracle of the Bridemere.

"He desired power and the return of true magic to our land, so he visited the Lady's Lake and peered into its depths by the light of the moon. No one heard what Bridelyn said to the Steward Taran that night, but all heard the despairing cry that tore from his lungs before he threw himself from the topmost window of the Mirror Tower.

"The Lake is the only true magic my people know now, though we still honor the legends of our great Dalrian mage kings and queens who perished long ago."

"But Steward, is not Bridelyn of the Mere one of those very mages? Does she not protect your people?" Rhyan asked.

"Indeed," he answered. "But in doing so, she seeks to keep us isolated and ignorant. She will use any means possible to achieve this end...including forcing the Steward Taran to take his own life."

"Your pardon," Rhyan said, sobered by his tale. "I did not mean to question your wisdom. I fear my recent injury has left me with wounded manners."

A smile lifted the corners of Morgan's stern mouth. "Well spoken, Lady Rhyannon. But it is I who should ask your pardon. To keep you standing and waiting in my hall—and you a guest overcome with pain? I can never do enough to repair my honor in this matter."

She returned his smile. "Please, my Lord Steward. I have taken no offense. In all honesty, I was bent upon the swift pursuance of our quest and tried to ignore all obstacles—even my own pain and exhaustion. My sister's life hangs in the balance, my lord, and the lives of many others."

He nodded. "The First Son and I have discussed the matter of the Kirrin's prophecy and your visit to the Bridemere. I fear we are not in agreement. Is it truly wise to pursue such a course? Is she likely to aid you in any way when, pardon my coarse words lady, the last foul son of the Trallendon house is in your company?"

The secret is out.

"I know somewhat of your history, my lord. Much of what I have learned, Keven of Tralleigh himself taught me. He told me of the nobility of your ancestors. He spoke honestly to me and placed blame for the great tragedy of your ancient war squarely on his own shoulders. I believe he is an honorable man.

"As to the question of visiting the Bridemere, we must insist! A terrible evil will be unleashed upon our lands unless we soon find the means to stop it. And my sister—I cannot bear to lose her."

"Peace, Chosen, I understand the bond of family. But I do wonder, how is it that you have been sent on this quest?" He shook his head, clearly perplexed. "Could not a warrior—"

"By the Crown of Teldar! I did not ask to be chosen!" Rhyan blurted out. "My sister was kidnapped by this madman and somehow the path to free her has led me here with the future of the Five Kingdoms of Valles hanging over my head."

"I meant no offense." Morgan bowed. "It is only that it seems a heavy burden to have placed on a lady so young...and beautiful."

Rhyan's face flushed at the compliment. She looked away from the Steward, only to meet Ailem's questioning gaze.

Her blush deepened. "You flatter me, my lord—though I expect the ladies of your kingdom rarely act with such little grace as I have. I do beg pardon, again. My sister is always telling me that my temper will get me into serious trouble someday."

Oh, Elspeth.

"I shall bring you some water, Chosen." Fiona picked up a large pewter jug from the bedside table and left the room.

Ailem stepped forward. "My Lord Steward, the *Chosen* requires as much rest as possible before our journey continues."

"Of course." Morgan extended his hand palm upward toward Rhyan. "Until tomorrow, Rhyannon Kember."

She pressed two fingers of her left hand into the Steward's palm. A burst of white light radiated from the Eyestone.

Morgan pulled his hand away. "By the 'Mere—what is that?"

Ailem raised one thin eyebrow. "Magic, Lord Steward. It would seem that you are invited to join our company."

SEVENTEEN

Of Enemies and Allies

Just as Ailem finished telling the Steward what they knew about the Eyestone and how Rhyan had come to hold it, a hard knock sounded on the door of the chamber.

"Come!" Morgan called.

The man who entered possessed a scarred and hardened countenance. But he appeared so much like Morgan in person and dress that she knew he must be a member of the Steward's family.

"Chosen, First Son, this is my uncle, Garth macNeill. He oversees the defense of our lands and the training of our men in the arts of war."

"My lord." Garth macNeill ignored his nephew's guests. "One of our scouts has returned to the castle gates with a messenger."

"From which party was the scout, Uncle?"

"From the eastren party. The messenger who accompanies him claims to be an envoy from Kai Mostfa, leader of the Plainspeople."

Morgan turned to his visitors. "On your honor—Chosen

Rhyan Kember, First Son Ailem Suir—I beg you, give me your word that what we have discussed here will remain private until such time as I choose. I pledge to give you all the aid I can in your quest, but you must promise me this."

"Of course," Rhyan said.

Ailem nodded.

Bowing, the Steward left. Garth macNeill gave Rhyan a sharp look through narrowed eyes and then stalked out after his nephew.

"I think I know who causes our good Steward to wish the Eyestone's invitation kept secret," she said.

"I have no doubt you are correct," Ailem said.

Fiona returned with the jug of water.

"The kitchen workers were somewhat afraid of me." She poured a cup for Rhyan. "They scurried out of my path, whispering of magic and the Bridemere. The gracious old Cook herself finally assisted me. She is a most talkative lady and full of pride in the Steward. 'We're all some glad that it was him made head of the clan—if you catch my meaning, young lady,' she said to me. Unfortunately, I am afraid no one else would speak to me and I was unable to uncover what she meant by such a comment."

"We have met the Steward's uncle, Wyddandaughter," Ailem said. "I have little doubt that the woman spoke of Garth macNeill. We should watch him carefully."

"I also met young Hale and Tura of Alder in the kitchen, First Son. They say they are being treated with honor. They left Collen resting his leg in the guest quarters, and Keven stayed to watch over him. I told them they had made a wise choice—Keven should remain out of sight for the duration of our stay. They asked after the Chosen and wondered if you had any instructions for them."

"Please tell them to return the honorable treatment they have received," Ailem said. "We must say and do nothing that will compromise our situation here. We *must* visit the Bride-mere."

When Fiona left the room, Rhyan closed her eyes to gather her thoughts, but fell almost immediately into an exhausted, dreamless sleep.

When she wakened, Ailem bent over her, smiling.

Rhyan felt his warm breath upon her face. The line of his jaw begged for the caress of her hand. Again, the smell of him—like a musky pine spice—made her yearn to be closer. Afraid of the sudden throbbing of her heart, she flushed and shifted away, sitting up.

Long shadows stretched on the wall beside her bed. "Have you been here the entire time I slept?"

"A few hours only," he assured her. "The evening sun has just touched the tip of the great *Daeig* Mountain. The Steward's messenger brought word that our presence is requested at a meeting in less than an hour's time."

"What kind of meeting?"

"The messenger would say only that the Steward wishes us to attend. Morgan macNeill also sent these garments as a gift to you." Ailem motioned toward a table in the corner of the room.

A brief knock sounded, and Fiona entered.

"The Wyddandaughter will help you ready yourself and escort you to the council chamber," Ailem said. "I will collect Keven of Tralleigh."

Fiona started. "First Son! Is that wise? Surely it will harm our cause!"

"I agree." Rhyan stood. "It cannot be safe."

"Safe, my Soulfriend?" Ailem took her hand. "It is most assuredly *not* safe. And yet, I hope...I think it is a wise decision." He opened his mouth as if to say more, but then glanced at Fiona, pulled his hand away and left the chamber.

"Chosen, I think he—"

"Please, Fiona, I don't want to talk about it."

"As you wish."

Before helping Rhyan dress, Fiona made her drink some fragrant tea to ward off another headache. The Faerie spoke softly and employed a light and gentle touch as she brushed Rhyan's hair and arranged it into an elaborate braid without the use of pins. Then she examined her injured arm.

"Thank you for your kind attentions," Rhyan said. "I am sure I am nearly healed."

"I pray to the Goddess that you are." Fiona did not meet her gaze.

"Fiona?"

"I felt something pulsing beneath my fingers as I touched you," the Faerie said. "Your arm, your neck, everywhere. Keven was right. There is something in your blood. It is powerful, hot, and angry. It frightens me, Chosen. And I am not easily frightened."

Rhyan shivered. *You are one of us, golden-eyed dragon-child.*

Fiona helped Rhyan finish dressing. The woven, copper-colored shirt felt smooth and cool against her skin. Close-fitting leggings and a short tunic were fashioned of a different, coarser material.

"These are fine garments for a warrior." Fiona fingered the fabric. "Almost as good as Faerie-make."

Rhyan agreed. With no tassels or loose folds, the simply cut blue and green plaid tunic would allow for full range of movement.

In the polished silver mirror over the chamber basin, she looked into the face of a strong, beautiful, and thoughtful young woman. The Eyestone picked up the copper hue of the shirt and accentuated the golden irises of her eyes.

Something lay hidden behind those eyes.

"I don't look like myself."

"Who is it that you see in the mirror, Chosen?" Fiona asked.

"I don't know. Someone older...and wiser."

The Faerie put her hand on Rhyan's shoulder. "I see a

woman grown and ready, Chosen. Come, we must go. The meeting will soon begin."

Bodies packed the Steward's council room. As Rhyan and Fiona entered, Tura emerged from the crowd.

"The Steward has reserved a seat for you at the table." She motioned Rhyan toward the center of the room.

Fiona led her forward. The Dalrians stepped back, leaving a clear path.

They fear us.

Seated at the large, circular table in one of only a few empty chairs, Rhyan indicated the one next to her. "Sit here with me," she said to Fiona.

"No, Chosen, I will sit along the wall near Hale Plendraig and Collen William's son. These seats are for the First Son and Keven Tralleigh."

Rhyan stifled a tremor of apprehension. From their attire, most of the Dalrians present appeared to be warriors. How would they react when Keven entered the room?

A very old woman, seated directly across the table, drew Rhyan's eye. Iron-gray braids formed a tight knot at the back of her head. She wore a plaid tunic—like Rhyan's, but a golden brooch adorned her shoulder, similar to the Steward's silver one. When her pale gray eyes met Rhyan's amber gaze, she inclined her head in respectful acknowledgement.

"Raaargh!" A young warrior sitting next to the old woman growled. He fixed an angry look upon someone who approached the table to Rhyan's right.

Keven of Tralleigh.

"What right does this *ciontach* coward have to sit at this table?" The warrior stood land slammed his fist down.

"My good sir," Ailem answered, "it was I who brought Keven of Tralleigh to sit with this council."

"And who *or what* are you?" The warrior growled, reaching for his weapon.

"He is Ailem Suir, First Son of Faerie." Morgan's voice

boomed out from the chamber entrance. Rhyan turned but could not see him. "He is my guest and a prince among his people, Blake Donnell. Offer him an apology or you'll have a seven-night in the stocks to think about it."

Donnell's face turned a mottled shade of purple, but he mumbled a few words and offered a stiff bow before taking his seat.

"As for Keven of Tralleigh, I cannot deny to you all that his presence unsettles me." Morgan continued to speak as he made his way to the table. "But I have discovered that Bridelyn herself allowed him across the river onto our lands. I think that none here would go against *her*."

A disgruntled murmuring broke out among the warriors as the Steward took a chair near the old woman and then motioned toward the door.

A tall, bronze-skinned warrior entered. She wore a tight, one-armed tunic of dusty brown and carried an ornate but well-worn bow. This she placed on the table as she sat next to Morgan. A patterned, woven band of copper and yellow held dark hair back from her strong-featured face, and a sunburst tattoo marked her bare shoulder.

"Let us begin." Morgan's command captured the attention of everyone in the room. "I have called this meeting to discuss the unsettling report of a marauding army loose on our borders. We know not their origin, but they have killed many of the Plainspeople."

The room erupted in shocked exclamations and questions. *Could it be Druin and the Dark Knight? How will we fight an entire army?*

"How do we know this information to be true, my lord?" Garth macNeill's loud, harsh voice silenced the tumult.

"The message is reliable," Morgan answered.

His uncle eyed the Plainswarrior and smirked. "Begging your pardon, my lord, but the word of a frightened girl isn't enough for me."

"Sure enough!" Blake Donnell burst out laughing. "Maybe the wee thing mistook a pack of wild pigs for monstrous creatures."

A few chuckles sounded around the table.

"Silence!" Morgan shouted. "What has happened to the hospitality of Dalria this day? Since when do we insult and deride honored guests and neighbors?"

The Plainswarrior stood. Her dark gaze narrowed on Garth macNeill.

"Peace, Steward of Mormar." Her accented speech rolled the "r" sound. "Dogs will bark at those they do not know." Some of the Dalrians covered their smiles and tried not to look at Morgan's uncle.

Garth macNeill clenched his hands into fists.

"I am no frightened girl," the warrior continued. "I am Kel Dana, sister of Kai Mostfa, chieftain of the Kanesga people. I passed the warrior tests four summers past and have taken the Night Ride no less than ten times. I am as skilled in the arts of war as any who sit around this table, and if challenged, I will prove my prowess to all here."

"Baagh!" Garth macNeill turned his head and spat on the floor.

Kel Dana put a hand to the long knife she wore at her waist.

"Uncle, I demand an apology on behalf of our guest." Morgan stood beside the Plainswarrior.

Garth locked eyes with his nephew in bold defiance, but at last looked away and fixed his still-heated gaze on Kel Dana. "Your pardon, my lady."

Rhyan sensed the untruth in his words. And the hatred. They grated on her senses like the scrape of metal against bone.

Morgan returned to his seat. "Please, Kel Dana, tell us what you have seen."

"Some time past, my brother received messages from two of our northren chieftains. They reported the loss of many *betan* to a large predator of some kind. We eat the *betan's* flesh, make cheese from its milk, warm clothing from its wool, and use the tanned hide to make *macracs*. A loss of fifty of these animals is a great hardship.

"My brother sent a large party of hunters and warriors to aid the villages in tracking down whoever—or whatever was responsible.

"Fourteen days passed, but my brother heard nothing. The villages sent no further messengers and our hunting party did not return. Another party was assembled and this time I was honored to lead it."

She is the kind of woman I want to be. Strong. Respected.

Kel Dana fingered the string of her bow. "Dun na Tur was a thriving settlement of three hundred families. They kept nearly six hundred head of *betan*. But we found only scraps of clothing, bits of horn and fur, and a few pools of dried blood. Strange prints marked the trampled ground. Even the wise old hunter I had brought with me could not identify the tracks.

"We spent the night in the empty village. In the morning, I sent word back to my brother, telling him what we found and that we were heading toward the other village. I hoped to find survivors there.

"My hope was in vain. Dun na Gol was just as empty, but this time the pools of blood were fresher. As night fell, my scouts found a large, unknown army camped just over the hills beyond the village.

"I went to view this marauding band that had slaughtered my people. Over a thousand fires lit the night. The scouts and I crept closer to view the three fires on the edges of the encampment.

"Around the first blaze I saw foul creatures—beasts standing on two legs—gray wolves, tusked boars, mountain cats and the like. They shouted to each other with harsh barking noises. At the second fire I saw tall, thin beings cloaked and hooded in dark crimson. They did not speak at all. I saw only their white, long-fingered hands glowing in the firelight.

"An armor-clad warrior sat in a princely chair next to the flames of the third fire. Sleeping around him were a dozen of the largest black wolves I have ever seen. The warrior's face washed red as he gazed into the fire. His lips moved as though he prayed to some evil god.

"I signaled to the scouts and was about to move away when a flicker of darkness in the flames caught my eye. I saw a shape emerging there. It was like a ghost—just the spirit of a thing that lived elsewhere. The apparition rose up, up—high above the campfire. Red and glowing, it writhed and twisted in the darkness until it filled the night sky like a spectral cloud. It spoke, and I felt its power.

"It was a *dragon-lord*."

The Dalrian warriors erupted into chaos. Shouts rang out from the corners of the council room and the clanging of drawn weapons echoed.

Across the table, the old woman fixed her gaze on Rhyan.

EIGHTEEN

The Bridemere

Ailem stood. "I ask to speak now, Lord Steward."

Morgan pounded his hand repeatedly on the council table. "Silence!"

"I add my words to those of Kel Dana," the First Son of Faerie said, once the disorder subsided. "The dragon-lord Druin is real. Through evil blood magic he is both man and dragon—a distortion of nature to be abhorred by all! My people have long feared that he would again call forth his corrupted minions to war against the Five Kingdoms. These abominations are no strangers to our lands. Your own people sent a force to aid the men of Kember and Windover during the time of the dragon-lord's first war. Surely the tale of Broch Fraser is still one told around your hearths? Did he not speak of *men of bones* and *foul were-beasts* when he returned here and recounted his great deeds? Did he not tell how he slew the boar-headed chieftain?"

"*Broch's Lay* is a tale to frighten children on a winter's even'," came a shout from the back of the room. One or two other voices called out, "Aye."

Murmurs and shifting of feet drew Rhyan's notice. Could it be that the rest of those present believed Ailem and Kel Dana?

"And what say you, Dougal Fraser, chief of your clan?" The gray-haired woman spoke at last, her voice soft and yet commanding. "What do you know of the lay of Broch Fraser?"

A heavy-featured, dark-haired warrior cleared his throat and leaned back in his chair. "The lay is a true tale," he rumbled, running a thick-fingered hand through his beard. "In my home, I have a manuscript written in Broch's own hand. It calls the evil beings *Dreadspawn* and describes them exactly as the Plainswoman has."

"It is easy to see what is required of us," the old woman said. "Are we not trained in the ways of war? Are we not strong? Do we not keep the winterbeasts from our doors each cold season? So must we also drive this horde away from our lands and our neighbors' villages. If they overcome the Plainspeople we will no doubt be next."

She paused, her unwavering gaze on Morgan. "So, Steward, will you sound the horn of war?"

A heavy, expectant silence filled the room. All eyes turned toward Morgan as he addressed his warrior council.

"My father's mother speaks true," he said. "This is more than a matter of honor. It is one of safety for our families. How do you vote, clansmen?"

"Fraser!" Dougal Fraser shouted as he rose to his feet and pounded his fist on the wooden table.

"Scott!"

"macClure!"

"Duncan!"

"Gowan!"

"macTavish!"

"macDonnough!"

A look passed between Blake Donnell and Garth macNeill before the younger man rose to his feet.

"Donnell," he said.

"macNeill!" Morgan's voice filled the room. "The call to war has been answered. Let each man here return to his house and put it in order. We leave in two days' time."

Wooden chairs scraped on the stone floor as the warriors hurried to begin their tasks.

"Shall I see to the weapons and provisions for the Steward's clan?" Garth macNeill asked.

"At once." Morgan's sharp blue eyes stayed glued to his uncle until the older man left the room.

"He means to give you trouble, Grandson," the dowager Lady macNeill said.

"He will honor my position, my *seanmhair*, though he does not approve of my methods."

Ailem touched his host's arm. "Pardon me, my lord Steward. I must insist that we visit the Bridemere as soon as possible."

"Peace, my friend," Morgan responded. "It is my wish that you do so. This eve we will meet at the foot of the Mirror Tower."

Lady macNeill's voice echoed in the emptying hall. "When the moon shows her face on the water—that is the time of prophecy. Then shall we hear the words of the royal Bridelyn."

Rhyan shivered.

Dusk fell into night. The milky, mottled waning crescent of the moon rose over the Bridemere, casting its reflection on the quiet water. Just below the Mirror Tower, Rhyan and her companions ranged themselves along the shore of the lake. The Dalrian warrior lords watched and waited a few paces behind, with Garth macNeill at their head.

Rhyan gazed at the smooth, glassy surface of the Bridemere. Her heart beat a constant staccato in her chest and a strange, itchy heat crawled under her skin. Out of the corner of her eye, she saw Ailem—on her right—make room for the Steward's lady grandmother at the water's edge. Morgan nodded to his *seanmhair* as he and Kel Dana of the Plains took places on Rhyan's left. Keven, Collen, and Hale stood just behind her.

"The hour has arrived," said the dowager Lady macNeill.

A white glow shimmered deep within the lake. A prism of dancing color broke the surface and a collective gasp arose behind Rhyan. The figure of a woman moved within the aurora. Silver-white hair swirled about a pale face, and dark blue eyes caught the light like faceted gemstones.

A cold drop of sweat trickled down between Rhyan's shoulder blades just as the pale lips opened.

"Why have you come?" The rebuke in the woman's voice rang like the harsh clanging of a sour bell.

"Excuse us, lady." Rhyan found her own voice rather like the chirp of a tiny bird compared to that of the fearsome specter hanging over the water. "We have been sent by the Kirrin to hear your words. Our land is in danger."

The cold lips moved into the shape of a smile. "Well am I aware of your danger, daughter. Have I not already spoken of it in your dreams?" The apparition answered in a softened tone. "You must be tired and distraught." A skeletal hand reached out and Rhyan suddenly felt so...so drained. The blue-diamond eyes became liquid. "My child, is this quest too much for you? You must surely need rest and a mother's care."

A mother. Rhyan closed her eyes. *A mother's soothing voice. A soft hand on her hair. The smell of lavender. A warm embrace...*

"Agh!" A jerk of pain brought her awake as Keven of Tralleigh reached out and twisted her arm.

"Rhyan Kember, do not fall under this dream spell," he whispered. "Bridelyn will spin a magical, mind-numbing web of glamour to ensnare her enemies."

"Enemies?" The bell rang sharper now as Bridelyn overheard him. "Had I ever more than one? This girl and her companions are not my enemies. A disease was my only enemy. A clinging, grasping, choking disease in a false guise. The sickness of love."

"Bridelyn." Keven seemed to age another hundred years as he said the name of his beloved. "Do not speak of our love as a disease. The hatred between our peoples and the cruelty of time—those were and *are* our only enemies."

The blue-gem eyes grew brittle-bright. Bridelyn floated toward them across the frothing water. "Ha! Even after so many years your silver tongue still twists words."

Keven dared to smile. "We were always well-matched in the magic of the voice."

"Well-matched? Do not speak of—"

"In the name of the Kirrin, Lady Bridelyn, you are compelled to give us your prophecy." Ailem stepped forward, interrupting the conversation between the fate-crossed lovers.

Bridelyn jerked back as if pulled by an invisible string. A slow whirlpool formed around her.

Her ringing voice now dripped with danger. "Noble Faerie lord, glean what you can from my vision. I tried to warn your Chosen. I give you not only the path to salvation, but also the way to destruction.

"Star Rider must gaze into Bridelyn's Mere
At midnight by moonrise pay heed to the seer.
Visions false, visions true
Which choice will the past undo?
River of death, secrets told
All paths lead to innocence sold.
Under the moondark sun, warriors meet their fate.
In the labyrinth beneath the mountain, evil and truth await.
Blood of the Goddess or power's call?
Dragon-child betrays all."

The swirling water stilled. A shining orb rose from the depths and hung in the air between Bridelyn and the watchers on the shore. Vision-images formed within.

Red-cloaked youth and silver-haired princess embrace and kiss. They ride together through whitestone gates.

Windhooves gallop over fields of grain, chasing a cloud of

boiling evil.

Sun disappears behind the moon. In the Tor's shadow, armies meet.

Dark arrows fly toward valiant hearts. Many fall.

Three starred swords clash—two of silvered steel, the third, midnight black. One blade shatters.

A dripping knife, a hooded figure, a still and bloodied blond-haired girl. A voice whispers, *'It was the only way....'*

Twisted metal gate opens. Seven jeweled circles wait.

Red dragon escapes across the sea.

Hundreds of bodies cover the ground.

Golden-eyed queen on a throne made of bones. Golden-haired girl stands at her side.

Eyestone flares, pierces its bearer's dark soul, reveals writhing serpents. The stone dissolves.

Prism-scaled dragon breaths white fire.

'You are one of us, dragon-child.'

No!

The images faded, and the orb sank.

Bridelyn's eyes met Keven's, then she vanished into the Bridemere.

The icy teeth of the frigid wind bit Rhyan's cheeks, bringing her back to the present.

No. No. A breath...two breaths.

It was the only way... Rhyan clutched the Eyestone. *Dragon-child betrays all.*

"Elspeth," she whispered.

"Chosen?" Fiona Wyddandaughter reached out a hand.

"Don't touch me."

"Not all of these visions will come to pass," Ailem said. "Bridelyn said so herself."

"Then why did we come here?" Rhyan shot back. "Of what purpose is it to let her show us lies?"

Will I betray my friends? Is that the only way to save my sister?

"Rhyan Kember, did you see my lost love and me?" Keven

asked. "Did you see our embrace? Our kiss? That is truth—an image from my own memory. I can still feel her hair beneath my hands." He stared down at his empty palms. "I am old. So very, very old.

"But we never entered the whitestone gates of Dalria together. Why was that shown? What does it tell us? An answer lies there."

Morgan of Dalria cleared his throat. "The vision shows some things clearly. Firstly, that we will meet the forces of Druin on the day of the darkened sun—just four days hence. The battle will take place in the shadow of Windover Tor. The Bridemere showed my own weapon, so I know my fate is tied to that battle." He drew his sword and held it high, the three starbursts etched along the blade glittering in the bright moonlight. "I will meet this challenge. I will stand against the dragon-lord—for my land and my people! What say you, First Son of Faerie?" The Steward thrust his free hand toward Ailem.

The First Son clasped it without hesitation. "I say that the blood of valiant Dalria runs true in thee, my friend. And I am proud that the white emeralds of Havenhome will fight alongside you." Drawing his jeweled sword, he raised it next to the Steward's blade.

Many of the watching warriors of Dalria gasped as they saw the two silver swords of the vision together.

Rhyan knew who held the black-starred sword. She knew who waited for them on the battlefield.

'Join us, golden-eyed dragon-child.'

She closed her eyes, tried to ignore the growing fire in her veins, and saw again the blood in her sister's hair.

It was the only way...

NINETEEN

Dun Na Riogh

Rhyan received a visitor early the next morning. Although fully dressed, she still blushed as the Steward's grandmother watched the maid brush and braid her hair.

The dowager waved the servant from the room and approached Rhyan. "I've brought you something." She held out a worn, leather-bound book.

"I am honored, my lady." Rhyan accepted the gift with a respectful nod.

"It is a copy of *Broch's Lay*. I'm guessing a young woman's education in Kember didn't include descriptions of the brutes and monsters you may face on this journey."

"You are correct, for the most part, my lady." Rhyan dared a small smile as she met the stern old woman's gaze. "Will you sit?" She motioned toward a bench against the wall. "I did have some lessons with a wise friend who lived near my home. Man Lyr told me—"

"Man Lyr?" The dowager Lady macNeill sat down abruptly. "Was he a friend of the family, this wise man?"

"Do you know him?" Rhyan asked.

The old woman regarded her for a few long, silent moments. "No good comes from magic—remember that, my girl."

She does know him.

"I brought the book so that you will be prepared for what you see. My grandson is the true heir to the stewardship and gives you aid that others would not, were they in his place. If you hold the power they say, I want you ready to use it to do what you must. I want Morgan to come home. I want him to remain the leader of our people. Do you understand?"

Rhyan nodded. *And I want my sister back safe.*

The dowager stood. "I have a feeling that, if I am still alive when this is over, I will see you in Rath Mormar again." She inclined her head in farewell. "Good luck, *Chosen*."

Rhyan thought over the encounter as she and Starlight rode alongside the Steward and Kel Dana over the Wizard's Bridge toward the Kanesga Plainsland.

What did she know about Man Lyr that she didn't want to tell me?

"This bridge was also built by the Dalrian mages," Morgan said.

"It's beautiful!" Rhyan marveled at the smooth whiteness of the stone, fashioned into two pairs of arms reaching out from opposite sides of the cold River Wenden, hands clasped to opposite forearms.

"Those were friendlier times." Morgan nodded to the proud Plainswarrior riding beside him.

"Indeed." Kel Dana cast a quick flickering glance back at Garth macNeill, who led the host of Clansmen about to cross the bridge.

Rhyan followed her gaze.

Morgan's uncle sent a foot soldier down the steep bank to the raging river. The man filled his water skin and then began the difficult climb back up.

That's odd. We've barely begun. No one should need to refill a water skin yet.

"That man has little respect for me or my people, Steward," Kel Dana said.

Morgan's jaw clenched, but he nodded. "My uncle has no more respect for a woman warrior than he has for a studious young stripling who would rather gaze at the stars than plunge a spear into a young deer."

Kel Dana lifted her black brows. "Under my brother's rule, one such as your uncle would be watched closely, so that when he rebelled, he could be dealt a swift punishment."

Morgan sighed. "I understand that my uncle is coarse and feels me inadequate to my position, but he is of my blood and will not turn against me, I am sure."

"I did not say *if* he rebelled, Morgan of Dalria."

Remembering her conversation with the Steward's grand-mother, Rhyan agreed.

The booted steps of warriors and the clip-clop of horses and Windhooves walking on the white stone echoed across the landscape.

Starlight tossed his head. *'The breeze shifts.'*

Conversation among the marching men fell silent. An unsettling energy crackled on the chill air.

Tura and Hale rode up to join the Steward's party.

"I like this not." Tura's bright eyes scanned the grassy hill that blocked the view of the Plainsland beyond the bridge.

"What is it?" Rhyan asked.

The Fairie shrugged. "We are in the open here and that is always dangerous, but there is something else, something in the wind, I think."

Hale swallowed, lifted his chin and put his hand to his belt knife. "Well, I am ready for it."

A smile played on Tura's lips. "Are you indeed, young prince? I think, though, that I will speak to the First Son about some better weaponry for you. If we are to face a fight, you should have the proper tools to defend yourself."

"Aiii!" Kel Dana's sudden shout drew the attention of all three thousand clansmen and those who rode with them. The Plainswoman rode swiftly across the remaining length of bridge. She drove her mount to the crest of the hill. Rhyan and her companions followed close behind.

Purpling waves of grass rippled across the vast expanse of flat land, unbroken save for a few stands of ochre flamebush. But a plume of thick black smoke rose in the distance. Rhyan caught her breath.

"A grass fire?" Morgan asked.

"No," Kel Dana answered. "I smell fighting and fear. *Hieeeeee!* I ride to Dun na Riogh!"

"We go with you!" Morgan wheeled his mount, signaling his uncle.

"*Chicaneg kask illaoa*! Fly like the wind!" Kel Dana yelled as her mount thundered down the rise and out onto the flat land. Rhyan and her companions followed, while Garth macNeill and his men brought up the rear.

A cold, noxious wind sprang up across the plain. It snatched Rhyan's breath.

'This wind is wrong,' Starlight told her.

How, my friend?

'I am a young Windhoove, Chosen, so I have not the lifewords to match my feeling, but the wind tastes sour...like sickness and rotting things.'

Rhyan glanced to the left and caught the eye of Tura's mount, Darkmane. He tossed his head and nickered.

'Darkmane says there is blood and...death.'

Gooseflesh pricked Rhyan's arms as she urged Starlight forward. The cloud of black smoke grew to fill the eastren horizon, hanging close to the earth like the hammer of a god about to strike.

"We are too late," Rhyan whispered. She rested one hand

over her chest where the Eyestone lay beneath her tunic.

A flush of warmth and then a sudden, shooting pain pulsed through her body. She swayed and would surely have fallen if Starlight had not been carrying her.

'*You are powerful, dragon-child.*' The Dark Knight's voice filled her mind. "*Embrace your anger. Become yourself. Bring us the Eyestone! We wait for you.*'

"No." Rhyan spoke low, beneath her breath. Her chest heaved. Droplets of sweat ran down her forehead into her eyes. Starlight's questioning concern sounded in her mind, but she blocked her thoughts and pushed against the heat rising inside.

Is this power evil? I won't give in to it, I won't!

With a rush, the heat faded, and the Eyestone lay cold and motionless against her chest.

Starlight galloped onward, bearing her toward Dun na Riogh.

On and on they ran. Minutes passed, then hours. At last, they entered Kel Dana's village. Hot, acrid smoke stung and scratched at Rhyan's already swollen throat. The smell of burning flesh made her want to retch.

All around, the warriors of Dalria dismounted in silence. Their drawn swords hung limp in their hands as they searched for signs of life. Dougal Fraser bent over the charred bodies of a man and woman lying hand in hand. He rose slowly, shaking his bowed head.

I could have saved them! If I had used the power. I could have...

"There must be someone left alive," she said.

"Rhyan." Ailem's voice and face betrayed no emotion. "It is unlikely—"

"I don't care what you say!" she shouted. "Don't you feel anything for these people? Are they just part of the quest—a step toward fulfilling the prophecy?"

Collen put his hand on her arm. "You're tired, lady. Come down from Starlight's back."

"No!" She swung her fevered gaze around the silent village.

Kel Dana knelt near the still form of a Plainswarrior pinned to the ground by a spear. His arm bore a white sunburst tattoo.

Her brother. Heat erupted inside Rhyan again. This time, she did not fight against it! She let the scorching pain and jagged anger tear through her body. The Eyestone burned like fire beneath her tunic. It drew her forward. This time, she opened herself, letting the hot rage and power take her into its rough embrace.

To the south, Starlight!

The Windhoove galloped forward, dodging between still-burning huts. With fleet hooves, he leapt over the dead of Dun na Riogh. Rounding a paddock filled with slaughtered *betan*, he carried Rhyan past a line of small storage shelters on the outskirts of the settlement.

In the distance, the smudge of the escaping Dreadspawn army moved across the horizon. Rhyan clenched her teeth. She coiled the hot center of her anger around the throbbing pulse of power that grew in her chest. As she urged Starlight to pursuit, a slobbering growl snapped her attention back to the village. A large, grass-covered mound rose from the flat ground not twenty paces away. Near it, a huge beast—a sharp-tusked boar—rooted at the mound and tore away the sod.

Power surged inside Rhyan like a flood-swollen river. A muffled sound echoed in her head. Far away someone wept and cried. She pulled the Eyestone from beneath her tunic and shouted as a burst of white-hot flame shot between her fingers and struck the beast. Like an arrow of lightning, it clove through the flesh of the dark thing, striking it in the heart. The smoking corpse dropped to the earth.

Rhyan leapt from Starlight's back. She yanked and pulled at the grass of the mound, only vaguely aware of the others as they caught up to her. Kel Dana's cry rang out as if from a great distance. Only when someone pulled Rhyan up from the ground and held her tightly did she return to herself. Tura helped the Plainswarrior lift the sod that had hidden the door of the mound.

Inside, two score Kanesga children held up their hands to shield their weeping eyes from the bright sunlight.

"Alive," Rhyan whispered.

Kel Dana turned toward her and raised her hands toward the sky. "*Tikal, tikal, tikal*! Praise and thanks, Chosen!"

"It was...the Eyestone." Rhyan swayed. The pulse of power subsided in dizzying waves. "It led me here. It killed the monster."

The Plainswoman reached out a hand to steady Rhyan. At her touch, the Eyestone glowed with a silvery white light.

Rhyan lost consciousness.

TWENTY

War Council

Once Rhyan woke, she immediately went in search of Kel Dana. She found the Plainswarrior standing over her brother's broken body. Kel Dana did not weep, but made a paste from the ashes of her village and painted her face with black symbols.

"This is my brother's name, and this, my promise to remember him as long as I draw breath," she told Rhyan, pointing to one cheek and then the other.

At the Plainswoman's direction, the clansmen of Rath Mormar dug a long succession of shallow pits along the west end of the village's barrow field.

"We will give each of the dead of Dun na Riogh the honor of a *camaliach*—a warrior's burial," she said.

Rhyan and her companions helped the children of the village paint the faces of their dead and then surround each body with the items needed for the trip to the afterlife. The older Plainschildren moved slowly among the bodies, quiet and emotionless as they marked the burned and tortured faces of family and friends with the white symbols of farewell. The youngest looked through the charred remains of homes, searching for personal items important to those who had died.

One child, a small boy whose face still held a babyish roundness, approached Kel Dana carrying a small drum with a broken head. "Dana-takan, do you think Menkara will want his drum with him? It is ruined."

Kel Dana knelt and put her hand on the boy's tousled dark hair. "How clever of you to find it, Kishu. Of course, Mankara will want to take the drum. It was his favorite. And remember, all things are made new in the Fields of Silverwind." The child smiled and ran back to his gruesome work.

Rhyan choked back tears.

With the dead made ready, she accompanied Kel Dana as the grief-wearied Plainswarrior walked among the shallow graves, whispering the prayer of leave-taking over each of the fallen. The clansmen of Rath Mormar watched in awkward silence, waiting to build the mound over each grave.

As the day ended, the Plainsvillage of Dun na Riogh put aside its mourning and became the encampment of an army. Over five hundred Plainswarriors arrived from outlying settlements to gather beneath the sunburst banner.

At Kel Dana's invitation, Rhyan and her companions joined the children of Dun na Riogh around a large campfire at the village center. The survivors shared a solemn feast of dried meat and hard bread.

Guilt washed over Rhyan. *How many would never eat again?*

After the meal, she and Ailem volunteered to watch over the children for the night. As they settled in, Ailem told her he had sent Kara Falcon to deliver word to the Faerie of the Old Forest.

"But aren't they too far away to help?" The sunset had brought a chill breeze and she shivered as she asked the question.

Ailem put his cloak around her shoulders. She leaned against him, overwhelmed and exhausted.

"The Windhooves will run without rest and bring them with

the dawn, Rhyan," he said. "They need not go to Rath Mormar, as we did, so their trip will be shorter."

Rhyan recalled the map she had seen in *Eadarowan*. As she tried to trace the route the Fairie would take, she fell asleep listening to the sound of Ailem's heart.

The voice of the Dark Knight echoed at the edge of her dreams.

She woke at first light, just as two full companies of Fairie and their Windhoove mounts entered the ruined village. Ailem had already risen to greet them.

The Fairie declined the offered breakfast of toasted bread and hot *haccano*, a strong, tangy beverage the Plainspeople brewed from holly bushes. Instead, they erected a large tent of whitewood and *alamathra* silk.

"It will house our war council," Ailem told her.

Morgan macNeill spoke to those seated around the table inside the tent some hours later. "Less than three days remain until the moondark falls upon the noon sun." He pointed to a large map of Valles hung on the wall. "Before sunset we will begin our march to the North Ford of the River *Eiren*. We cannot cross at the Great Bridge—our scouts have informed us that it is held by three score of the Prince of Windover's finest archers. They sit on the heights and would pick us off as we crossed, neat and sure."

"Is it safe to cross into the North Kingdom?" Kel Dana asked. "Our shaman tell strange tales about the abandoned lands beyond the North Ford."

Ailem stood and nodded toward Morgan as he addressed the council. "The Faerie, too, have heard tales of the shades of the North Kingdom. The people of that lost time did not let go of this world easily. Many have denied themselves the peace of true death. We cannot expect to be left alone as we cross that haunted land."

"It matters not what misted shades lie in wait for us, Faerie-lord! We Dalrian clansmen do not travel cross-country to fight ghosts and goblins," Blake Donnell said. "We crave warriors of flesh and blood."

"The shades of the North Kingdom are all too real," Ailem responded. "They could test the courage of the bravest warrior."

"You insult me, *taobh a muigh*!" Donnell's hand went to his sword.

"Enough!" Morgan pounded his fist on the table. "I will have no more petty outbursts from my men. We shall all meet our true enemy face-to-face soon enough."

Donnell gritted his teeth but bowed his head and dropped his hand from his sword.

"What of the Chosen?" Garth macNeill asked from the rear of the council tent. "You say she used the Eyestone to slay the boar-beast with a single blow. Can she not remove Prince Evnis's archers? We could then use the Great Bridge to bypass the North Kingdom and save ourselves much time."

Rhyan's cheeks flushed as all eyes turned toward her.

What will happen if I give myself over to it again? Will I become evil?

"The Eyestone is an unpredictable weapon," Ailem said.

"Meaning that the Chosen cannot yet control its power." Morgan's uncle smirked, and then nodded in Rhyan's direction. "Begging your pardon, lady."

You're wrong. She wanted to shout in response, but instead she shrank into her chair. *It's the only powerful weapon we have and I'm afraid to use it!*

"Controlled or not, the ability to use the talisman is hers alone," Ailem said. "The Eyestone gives its power where it will. She is the bearer. She is the Chosen. Her role is set. She will enter the labyrinth and use the Eyestone to defeat Druin. Our goal will be to clear the way and hold off the Dreadspawn army until she succeeds."

But what if I accept the Knight's offer? Give the Eyestone to

Druin and he will expel the Dreadspawn. I can take over the rule of these lands. And save my sister.

Dragon-child betrays all.

"Well, then." Garth macNeill snorted and turned back to the map of Windover Tor. "Good fighting men will do what must be done."

I will do what must be done. I will meet Druin beneath Windover Tor. Flames of anger licked at the edges of her mind and the Eyestone tingled in answer.

Raised voices outside the tent interrupted Rhyan's thoughts. She shifted in her seat as a gray-cloaked man entered. The snow-white falcon perched on his shoulder spread its wings and cawed loudly as the council members rose to their feet.

Man Lyr?

Morgan cleared his throat. "Thank you for joining us, Mannawyddan. We are grateful for the power and wisdom of the White Wizard. Welcome *Calon-fawr.*"

Man Lyr shook his head. "It is well-known that my power is not what it once was, Steward. I paid a heavy price to trap Druin within the labyrinth. You must address me only as Man Lyr. I no longer hold rank and my wisdom is...such as it is."

Fiona left the council tent.

Speechless, Rhyan stared at her old tutor. *Man Lyr is Mannawyddan, the White Wizard of legend? Why didn't he tell me? Why hadn't he gone after Elspeth? Why did he send me alone to face the Glade and retrieve the Eyestone?*

"Your captains are more qualified than I to offer attack strategies and battle plans," Man Lyr said. "I tell you only that you must hold against the Dark Knight and his army as long as you can. The Chosen must be given time to reach the final gate—the Dragon's Gate—at the center of the labyrinth beneath Windover Tor. She alone holds the power to defeat Druin."

All eyes again turned toward Rhyan.

"Man Lyr, I–"

"She is our only hope," Man Lyr continued. "She has accepted her call. Now we must accept ours and allow her to fulfill her destiny."

"But must we cross at the North Ford?" Ailem turned his attention back to the map. "Is it safe to travel the barrowlands?"

"The northren way holds no danger for us," Man Lyr said. "It is the best choice since the Prince of Windover holds the Great Bridge."

Morgan cleared his throat. "Aye. We strike camp at once and march before noon."

"Man Lyr!" Rhyan called to the wizard as he left the tent with Morgan. "Man Lyr!" She ran after him and reached out to tug at the back of his cloak.

But before she touched it, he stopped and turned to face her. "Little Dragon?"

"I...I need to talk to you," she stammered.

"And I need to talk to you, alone, soon. Allow me time to speak to Morgan macNeill about our crossing of the Ford into the North. I will seek you out later." He turned and walked away.

Dismissed! Pushed aside like a troublesome child.

She looked for Ailem, but he wasn't among those still gathered nearby.

He wouldn't treat me with such condescension.

'Indeed, I would not, Rhyan.'

Starlight?

'No, it is I, Ailem. I must speak with my warriors now, but I will seek you out as soon as I am able.'

But how...?

'I have heard you on the edge of my thoughts for some time, but I have not had an opportunity to speak with you alone about it. I meant to tell you last even', but you fell asleep so quickly. It sometimes happens after the sharing of names, when a special magic grows between the sharers.'

A special magic? What do you mean?

'Have you not guessed, Rhyan-of-my-heart? I—'

"Lady Rhyan!" Collen jogged up beside her. "We must find Hale Plendraig and make ready."

"Yes, I'm coming."

Ailem?

'Be patient, Rhyan.' His words cooled her troubled spirit. *'We will speak soon.'*

As she followed Collen to the makeshift training yard Tura had set up on the outskirts of the camp, Rhyan wondered at Ailem's ability to hear her thoughts. How long had he been listening? Did he know of Druin's offer?

No. She'd been careful to keep those worries hidden from Starlight. Surely Ailem would have confronted her if he knew.

"He's a quick study, your cousin." Collen interrupted her thoughts.

She watched Hale finish a series of short sword thrusts and parries against his practice opponent. Sweat-streaked dust coated his face.

Why couldn't the Eyestone be as simple to use as a sword?

Collen left to fetch water and towels and Keven walked out to join Rhyan. "Young Hale has found a part to play, I see."

"Some parts are easier than others."

"Indeed. It is our own choices that cause the difficulties."

Rhyan closed her hand around the Eyestone. "Often we are not allowed to choose."

"We all make choices," Keven said. "We take certain paths and reject others. We pursue power without realizing the cost." His gaze turned westward. "Or we fight for freedom without knowing what that truly means. Sometimes we choose to do nothing. And that, my young friend, is the saddest choice of all."

TWENTY-ONE

Voices of the Dead

The makeshift army traveled northward and approached the Ford of the River *Eiren* as the sun sank behind the Westren Mountains. Darkness settled over the land and an eerie fog rolled across the river from the marshlands. Rhyan heard the tramp of hundreds of boots and hooves and the jingle of the Dalrian horses' reins, but she could barely see to the end of Starlight's nose.

How can you find your way?

'*I simply know it,*' Starlight answered. '*We tell our northren cousins since they have not our senses.*'

It's a miracle you haven't left hoof prints on a warrior or two.

'*These men are noise-makers. I would be deaf indeed to step upon one.*'

Rhyan giggled.

'*We have arrived at the crossing place,*' Starlight said as Keven and Tura rode out of the fog.

"She's here," Keven announced.

"Who?"

"Bridelyn."

"But, how? I thought she couldn't leave the waters of the River Briden and its branches and tributaries."

"I don't know. It shouldn't be possible, but I feel her spirit in the waters of the *Eiren*," he said. "She is here, and she will not allow us to cross." Keven lifted two fingers to his lips and gave a piercing whistle.

One by one, the others emerged from the fog. Ailem arrived last. Man Lyr rode at his side.

The two avoided Rhyan's gaze.

They've been talking about me.

"I see nothing," Kel Dana said, "but I feel eyes watching."

A sudden swirl of mist brushed against Rhyan's shoulder. She turned to find a clearing in the fog.

Bridelyn's shade hung over the middle of the shallow waters of the North Ford. "Stop!" she shrilled. "You shall not cross here—I forbid it!"

Morgan stepped forward and went down on one knee before the long-dead princess of Dalria. "My lady, as leader of your people, I most respectfully plead our case. We go to destroy a dragon-lord. If we fail, our people will suffer. Surely you would not keep us from our quest? We must bring the Chosen—"

"Aieeeee! Speak not of that girl to me. She has cast a spell of her own over all of you. You are blind to the evil seed of betrayal that germinates within her!"

"Bridelyn..." Keven's melodic voice carried over the water. "You bade me to choose and I have chosen to help this girl save our land from Druin. Would you countenance the murder of so many innocents? I cannot again face so much death."

"I, too, remember the death of innocents," Bridelyn responded. "Even in my half-life, I feel the weight of the destruction we caused. Do you not feel that burden, Keven? You did nothing to stop the horrors of war until I forced you into our vow. Why do you choose to act now, to aid and defend this girl, this dragon-child? She holds the possible doom of the world in her weak hands! I saved her from the foul Cumbrian knight and bid her turn away from this quest—away from the impossible choice that awaits. But she continued—you saw the vision in the Bridemere! She will embrace power and deliver Druin his key to freedom. She is darkness!"

Bridelyn reached out a ghostly hand.

A thick tendril of fog covered Rhyan's mouth. Her breath caught in her throat as Bridelyn's power yanked her from Starlight's back into the river.

The water ran winter-cold, but not deep. She watched, trapped and drowning, but strangely calm, from just beneath the shallow surface as chaos broke out among her companions.

Starlight took a step toward her, but his head butted against an invisible wall. Collen and Ailem jumped from the backs of their Windhoove mounts and tried to shoulder through the barrier on foot but could not. Man Lyr raised his hands and his lips moved—did he call out a spell? Bridelyn threw a powerful wave onto the bank and knocked him to the ground.

Pinpricks of light formed on the edges of Rhyan's vision. Her chest ached with the need for air, but Bridelyn held her frozen to the river bottom.

Keven dismounted. He dropped his hat and cloak onto the damp grass and walked to the water's edge.

"Bridelyn." The water muffled Keven's voice, but Rhyan still heard his words from beneath the surface.

"Don't plead for her life. I won't give it to you."

"I plead only for you, my love," Keven said. "I have missed you...these days since you released me."

Rhyan's hand broke the water's surface as Bridelyn's power wavered.

"Do not try to trick me."

"There is no trick here, Bridelyn. I care for this girl because she chooses to act, because she loves her sister, and because her spirit reminds me of you. And I have wondered what it would be like to hold your hand again."

He stepped into the water.

"Keven! Do not! You will die!" Bridelyn screamed.

"I am dead already. I have been dead these many years. What is life without love?" He dove into the river.

"Keven!" Bridelyn screamed. Her shade burst in a shower of ice diamonds.

Rhyan surfaced, gasping.

Ailem waded into the water and pulled her into the safety of his arms. His heart pounded against her cheek when she leaned into him.

'My love, my love.'

"I can't see him anywhere," Collen said.

"He's gone," Rhyan whispered. "Gone."

Ailem's embrace tightened. "It was his choice."

She pushed him away. "No one chooses to die!"

"No." Ailem brushed tangled, dripping hair out of her eyes. "But some may give their own lives to save those they love."

Midnight had come and gone by the time the army forded the river and entered the Northlands. As the fog cleared, strange shapes loomed up around them in the darkness.

"We'll stop here," Morgan ordered.

"What is this place, lady?" Collen rode up on Rhyan's left.

"A graveyard." A prickle of unease slithered along her spine. "Those are grave markers."

"This is *Barrowheim*, the royal burial yard of the old North Kingdom." Ailem dismounted. "Every ruler from King Semmuel the First to Queen Mirandrabeth, their last and greatest ruler, is buried here. Many barrows are unmarked or have gone to dust, but some still stand to greet us in the night.

"My Lord Steward," he called ahead to Morgan. "Passing through this place with reverence, I accept. But camping on ancient hallowed ground could be testing the strength of our grant of safe passage."

"If this ground be hallowed, First Son, then it can only be to our benefit. Our enemies are profane and evil. Mayhap this sacred soil would burn their tortured souls. Our wizard friend assures me that we may rest here in safety." Morgan motioned toward Man Lyr, who appeared suddenly out of the fog.

Like a ghost. Rhyan shivered.

After setting up camp, warriors gathered around their fires, readying weapons—and their courage—as they recounted old battle tales.

Rhyan walked past them to sit alone at a smaller fire. Collen followed and gathered wood to feed the blaze. But when Man Lyr arrived, the young man bowed to Rhyan and joined the others.

"I need to talk to you, Little Dragon."

Keven's death had left her numb, and yet her pulse throbbed with the heat of power struggling to come to life in her blood. Anger and power.

"Where were you?" Rhyan's voice cracked. "While I was being tested by the Faerie and attacked by the Dark Knight and failing to save the Plainspeople? Where?"

Man Lyr poked the end of a long stick into the struggling fire. The embers flared and crackled to life.

"I traveled to the home of my friend, as I said," he answered. "But I found her hearth cold and her bookshelves empty. One of her boats was also missing. I was concerned because she hadn't sent word that she intended a trip, but I had no time to search for her.

"Instead, I used what little magic I still possess to travel in spirit form to Windover Tor."

"And what did you find there?"

"All was as Kara Falcon reported. Druin's power grows as the enchantment weakens. And his servant of old is returned–"

"I know that servant well! The Dark Knight has been chasing me since I left your cottage." Rhyan's loud voice carried. Faces turned in their direction, lit yellow-orange by the firelight.

"We run out of time, Little Dragon," Man Lyr said. "I must

tell you of the labyrinth beneath the Tor."

Rhyan looked up at the stars blanketing the velvet sky. Again, familiar shapes offered comfort: Bilden—dimmed but still fully visible, the Arrow, and the North Cross. On this night, the Sisters burned brighter than she had ever seen them. The double-star joining their hands twinkled like a jewel turning in sunlight.

Man Lyr had taught her the constellations. She remembered nights on the roof of Caer Kember's tallest tower with a Watchguard as chaperone. When she saw the Sisters for the first time, she couldn't wait to tell Elspeth. Man Lyr had laughed at her excitement.

He was someone else then. And so was I.

"Why did Morgan macNeill call you *Calon-fawr*?" she asked.

He tossed another log on to the fire. "One of your forefathers, the prince who originally shed his blood over the Dragon's Gate, gave me that name. It means "Great-heart" in the ancient tongue of Kember. I was considered a hero for saving Valles from Druin—because I came when others did not, and because of what I lost."

Rhyan glanced toward him, but he leaned away from the firelight and she could not see his expression. "So, this labyrinth, is it like the hedge maze at Caer Kember?"

"A labyrinth is not a maze," Man Lyr said, "although some use the term interchangeably. Labyrinths are not puzzles made for amusement or protection of castles or manor houses. Nor do they have high walls, fences, hedges, or mirrored glass to confuse those who enter. Labyrinths have but one entrance and one path that leads to the center and then back out. They are meant to represent an inner journey."

"Did you make the labyrinth beneath Windover?"

He shook his head. "It was created long before my battle with Druin. When the wizards first came to Valles, they heard tales of the endless caves beneath the Tor. The villagers living nearby claimed that those who ventured beneath the mountain either returned mad or not at all.

"Llu, the most powerful of the ancient wizards, entered the caves to test the truth of the tales. He came out before the passing of an hour. 'A labyrinth,' he told us. 'An exact duplicate of the one built by Caeros in the City of Turnings—and *I am not ready to die.*' From that time until the trapping of Druin, none entered the caves of their own accord.

"As the oldest among us, Llu departed this plane long ago. But during my own studies at Veritannis, I discovered his journal. In it, he described the City of Turnings labyrinth—the Seven Circles of the Soul he called it—and detailed the dangers to be faced by any who attempted to travel it. The circuits of the labyrinth each had a gate, but no walls. Their floors were marked by paths of colored stone. Each circle's trial was represented by a color—one of the seven that make up the fabled prismed Path of the Soul. Llu explained that only a talisman blessed by the Goddess could pass the seventh gate—the final gate—into the center. I continued studying Llu's journals and the other ancient tomes in Veritannis and came to believe that, using living, Goddess-blessed blood of the Windover family, I could not only pass the seventh gate, but lock it, creating a prison at the center.

"When Druin Canwyr turned against our calling and attacked the people of Valles, I decided to use what I had found to trap him in the labyrinth. My spell worked, in a way. It allowed me to safely deliver him to the labyrinth's center. However, the blood price is an ancient law and is not easily altered to suit our needs. In my arrogance, I learned that lesson well." The old wizard's voice faltered. "Elina...Elina was wiser than I."

"Who was Elina?" Rhyan asked.

"She was a Faerie-wizard—the first born among her people—and a very old friend," Man Lyr answered. "My initial spell allowed her to accompany me into the labyrinth. Then, in the midst of casting the enchantment to create the *Dragon's Gate*—with the then-Prince of Windover's bleeding arm strapped to the entrance of the final circuit—I became exhausted...my mind fatigued beyond reason. All I could remember was the final spell. I had to complete it to lock the gate, but it would not close! I kept on repeating the words, kept drawing on the ancient power of the gate, kept calling on the latent power in the Prince's blood, but the spell would not close!

"Elina stayed back, watching and waiting."

"Waiting for what?" Rhyan asked.

"For our enemy to rouse. She sensed his power, weakened though he was, and she knew that he would wait until I was most vulnerable to strike. I had temporarily blocked his power over the elements. Through the shedding of his blood and the mingling of it with my own, I had blocked his use of all but the magic of transformation. What did it matter what form he took when I had bound all his other abilities beyond his reach? What harm could he cause as a beast? How arrogant I was. Druin raised his bloody arms and spoke that last horrible spell, changing himself into his current dragon form.

"It was then that Elina stepped before him. Using her own blood—her own lifeforce, she threw up a shield spell over the Prince and myself. She did nothing for her own protection. It was not through error that she left herself unguarded. She knew that the blood price had to be fully and truly paid. Elina... perished in the dragon's fire. And the spell closed, completed. Through her death, Druin was securely bound by my magic. She was the true hero. A selfless, beautiful soul.

"I lost most of my own power that day—the price of such an intricate enchantment. I left Windover, and many assumed that I had returned to dwell with my own kind on the hidden Isle of Wyde. But I had withdrawn to a simpler life, studying forest lore and teaching children.

"As time passed, the conflict with Druin faded into legend and life in the Five Kingdoms returned to normal. Many of the old bloodlines weakened over the years, but the Windover family stayed true. They honored the Time of Renewal and kept the enchantment strong."

"Why did you need the Prince of Windover's blood?" Rhyan asked

"The Windover line is the most ancient of all the human families in our land. They were leaders of their race and the first to arrive after the sinking of Isle Dyfed. In the past, they had given their lives to the nurture of the land and its people. In doing so, they had followed the path of the Goddess. Their power comes from her. It is blessed—a magic that rests within the soul. Unlike a wizard's or sorcerer's magic, which is the ability to draw power from other sources using the lifeforce contained in blood, the Windover family's magic is a power of place and belonging. Windover belongs to them, and they, to Windover.

"By using their blood, I was able to draw upon both the magic of wizards and the power of the Goddess. In this way, I hoped the enchantment would bind Druin forever.

"The *Dragon's Gift*—the part of the magic that remained in the Windover bloodline—allowed its bearer to safely pass through the circuits of the ancient labyrinth to the true center. Once there, a small, harmless amount of the bearer's blood would be spilled over the final gate. This would renew the enchantment for another ten years. It was truly a masterful piece of magic.

"Until Evnis, the *Dragon's Gift* had always passed to a firstborn son because that was the way that I had structured the spell.

"Somehow, Druin altered the *Gift*. Over the last few generations, he has been able to grow in strength and recover access to his magic, though his physical form has remained trapped at the center of the labyrinth—blocked by the *Dragon's Gate*."

"My uncle, the Prince, told us that he had been searching for a means to give himself the *Gift*," Rhyan recalled.

Man Lyr nodded. "Druin promised your uncle that the power would be his. He used that lie to persuade Evnis to bring your sister to him. Druin was simply using him and will never allow him true power of any kind."

"How can we be sure that Elspeth is still all right? My dreams are dark. And in Bridelyn's vision, my sister seemed...dead."

"Druin must have her alive at the Time of Renewal, Little Dragon. He must have the living blood of an heir to the *Dragon's Gift* to perform the ritual that will free him. You must be at the center of the labyrinth, with the Eyestone, when the moondark arrives. You must pass through each circuit of the labyrinth and face the visions that you see there without giving up the Eyestone! Only the Eyestone can truly defeat Druin."

"What will the visions show me?" Rhyan asked.

"I cannot tell, for I do not know," Man Lyr said. "They are different for each traveler."

"We will be in time, won't we?" Rhyan asked. "We will save Elspeth?"

"You must focus on destroying Druin, Little Dragon! That is our main goal and purpose. That is the only chance to save us all." Man Lyr pulled up the hood of his cloak, hiding his face. "You must reach the center of the labyrinth with the Eyestone." He rose and left the fire.

Rhyan peered into the flames. *Is anyone else thinking of Elspeth? If I take Druin's offer, I could save her. And I could be like Mirandrabeth. I could unite our lands in peace under one Overqueen. Expel the Dreadspawn and keep everyone safe. I'd be wise and strong and powerful.*

When she finally stirred, her stiff back and shoulders ached with cold. She moved closer to the fire. Collen brought her a blanket and a small sack of flour to use as a pillow.

"The First Son is in council with his people, lady Rhyan," he told her. "He said you should get some sleep."

"Were you listening to what Man Lyr told me?"

"Aye," Collen answered. "I beg pardon for it, lady."

"Don't apologize. It wasn't a secret meeting. What did you think of his tale?"

"I think we're all paying the price for choices made long

ago—you most of all, lady."

Rhyan sighed. "I set out to find Elspeth and bring her home. But now everything is so complicated. How do I know what's right?"

Collen sat down beside her. "It's easy enough to keep going along the same path with everyone else, plodding on like sheep to the watering hole. But it takes a brave heart to question the path and courage to choose our own way. My grandsire tells me to trust my own heart."

"But I think my heart is changing, Collen."

"I trust you, my lady," he said. "I will always trust you. You should trust yourself."

Would he trust me if he knew about Druin's offer?

"You should get some sleep, lady."

Rhyan accepted the blanket and pillow he'd brought. "I will, on one condition. Can you just call me Rhyan? No more 'my lady,' please."

He smiled. "I'll try...Lady Rhyan." He waited until she lay down, then left to check on the Windhooves.

The moon moved across the starred sky and disappeared behind distant clouds. But still, sleep would not come. Rhyan's thoughts raced with memories of Elspeth and Caer Kember, of the journey that had taken her far from home, of the way Ailem's breath warmed her skin, of Collen's honest words, and of the powerful thrill of wielding the Eyestone.

Power is what I want. To be in control...to command and make my own choices. To rule!

A whisper of wind blew a stray hair across her face.

'Chosen One...' A woman's voice echoed in Rhyan's mind.

Am I dreaming?

'Chosen...'

Rhyan stood and let the blanket fall to the ground. She peered out into the night but saw no movement. The entire camp seemed asleep.

'Chosen...'

The eerie, echoing voice drew her across the barrowyard. Strangely unafraid, she skirted campfires and stepped over sleeping warriors until she found herself standing before a magnificent spreading oak made of white stone. The tree glowed in the starlight. An arched doorway opened in the trunk. Recalling Man Lyr's teaching, Rhyan deciphered the runes carved above the entrance: *Mirandrabeth, last Queen of the North Kingdom.*

'Closer, Little Dragon...'

Rhyan peered into the doorway. Stone steps led downward and a misted light filled the interior of the barrow. She descended and crossed the wide floor to the royal sarcophagus. An effigy of the queen sat upright on an ornate throne perched upon the massive, ancient coffin. The eyes of the death mask opened and met her own.

I am dreaming.

The stone lips moved. "This is no dream, Little Dragon. I have called you here to give you warning." The voice paused as the statue's cold, emotionless eyes shifted to a dark area in the corner of the icy tomb.

Rhyan turned toward the shadows and watched, chilled to the bone, as the specter of a young girl slid soundlessly out of the damp, lichened stone wall and floated to the side of the North Queen.

"Lysana," the Queen whispered. "My daughter." The ghost child climbed into the arms of her dead mother's monument. The thin, white, transparent arms slipped around Mirandrabeth's cold stone neck.

"She was taken by a fever," the Queen said. "During her illness, I nursed her myself, willing her to live. She died in my arms. My only child."

"I'm so sorry," Rhyan said.

The Queen's stone lips turned upward in a slight smile. "Do not pity us, Chosen. Our spirits live in a place of peace. We roam on occasion, but in many ways, we are content. Yet, we cannot touch as we did before. Lysana misses it." She lifted a stone hand and caressed her ghost daughter's hair.

"I, too, miss my mortal existence at times. I, who took many secrets to my grave, give this small one to you, Chosen."

The dead Queen extended her hand and Rhyan reached out to catch the object that dropped from the cold fingers: a silver ring. In the semi-darkness, Rhyan could just make out the design of a simple labyrinth worked into the metal. A single tiny diamond marked the center. Rhyan slid the ring onto her finger.

"Keep my token, Chosen. It is not a weapon, as is the powerful talisman you wear about your neck. The ring is a symbol and key passed down through long generations to the heirs of the North Kingdom. Keep it and remember the dead North Queen and her daughter. Seek truth and do not be blinded by power. It is no surety against pain and loss. Wisdom lies at the center.

"The night grows old. I was given leave to give my gift and my warning. Take them and remember: I, too, was a daughter of magic, but I was blind to the power of truth. Do not, in your pride, turn from the Path of the Goddess as I once did.

"My time here is done this night," the Queen said. "Come, Lysana." The ghost-child tried in vain to cuddle closer to her mother.

"Thank you, Madame," Rhyan whispered.

"Be true to yourself, Chosen..." Queen Mirandrabeth's voice echoed as the light faded from the statue's eyes and Lysana's ghost returned to the shadows.

Rhyan stood alone in the darkness.

She felt her way up the stone steps, running her hand along the wall. As she exited the barrow entrance, Fiona approached, carrying a burning torch. The diamond of the labyrinth ring winked in the flickering light.

"Chosen?"

"Fiona! I heard a voice from the tomb and—is something

wrong?" In the flame-light of the torch, the Faerie woman's face appeared wild and angry.

"Yes, Chosen. When I heard you speaking to Man Lyr this evening, I felt my old hatred rushing to the very tips of my fingers. I went to the First Son and he counseled patience, speaking to me of Man Lyr's past service." The Faerie woman spat on the ground. "I decided that I could not keep the truth from you any longer."

"What truth, Fiona?"

"My mother was Elina of the Faerie."

"Elina? I know her story. Man Lyr told—"

"He *lies*, Chosen! He killed her! He says that she sacrificed herself, but he forced her to do so to save his own life. He was a wizard of vast knowledge—how could he not know that the blood price must be paid? The White Wizard killed my mother as surely as if he had taken his own knife and stabbed her."

"Fiona! Let us go to Man Lyr together and—"

"I will not, Chosen! I will not let myself be swayed by his lies as so many others have been. And his treachery is not only in the past. Who do you think will pay the price this time? Will it be your sister? Will it be you?"

"You are angry and hurt." Rhyan laid a hand on the young woman's arm. "But you can't know Man Lyr as I do. He would never—"

"Can't know him? How is it that I could not know my own father?"

"Your *father*?"

"When my mother died, he left me with her people. Because of him, I have lived a lonely life—looked down upon and excluded. The Faerie chose to forgive Man Lyr for his transgressions, but judged my mother an aberration and a renegade."

"But...wasn't your mother a wizard, too?"

"Yes, curse them all! That is why she was *eachrrannach*—an outcast. Unlike the forest magic of the Kirrin, the magic of the wizards is an unnatural thing to the Faerie. It sometimes requires innocent blood and often means the corruption or manipulation of the natural order—and transformation into beast or creature-things the Faerie abhor. Man Lyr is of ancient wizard stock and the Faerie long ago made peace with those who watch over our lands from the Isle of Wyde. But they could not accept that one of their own was wizard-kind. No one knows why my mother—a pure blood Faerie—was blighted in the womb with their magic."

"Fiona, are you—?"

The half-blood Faerie raised her hand to interrupt. "I am what I am, Chosen. It is who my father really is that should concern you."

TWENTY-TWO

The Dragon's Gate

A brisk wind clamored against the rocky foothills of Windover, like a multitude of voices lamenting the approaching conflict. From the top of the ridge, Rhyan gazed down at the impenetrable, roiling mass of black clouds covering the plain. The Dreadspawn army remained hidden beneath the thick fog.

The allied forces were gathered on the foothills. The men who had arrived from Kember and the Southlands waited near the tumbled stones of the ruined watchtower. Lord Angus Kember's blue hart banner flapped amidst those of the other noble families. Rhyan sent up a silent prayer to the Goddess for her uncle's safety.

The rest of the free peoples massed just above the line of black clouds. On the right flank, the Kanesga Plainswarriors gathered in tight circles. The hum of their chanting voices rose above the tearing wind. Kel Dana said they invoked the spirits of their ancestors, asking for aid in the coming battle.

The Dalrian forces held the center column. They stood, weapons in hand, as if eager to be the arrow point of the attack.

On the left, the Faerie waited on their Windhoove mounts. Some held battle bows, but most wore the familiar light-silver swords their people favored.

Rhyan sat on Starlight's back, with Ailem, Morgan, Collen, Tura, and Kel Dana gathered around her on their mounts. They waited for Man Lyr to arrive and accompany Rhyan to the tunnel and the caves where she would enter the labyrinth to meet Druin.

Where are Hale and Fiona?

Rhyan felt Ailem's eyes on her. She knew he listened to her inner struggle—at least the thoughts she allowed him to hear.

I am strong. I have power. I will rescue Elspeth! Tingling fire coursed through her veins. Ardent, wild, and uncontrolled, it grew with each passing minute.

"I *am* the Chosen," she breathed into the wind.

'*No one doubts you, my friend,*' Starlight told her.

'*All are here to aid you, Rhyan,*' Ailem comforted.

They doubted me at the war council. They will not doubt me again.

"How will we know when the moondark arrives?" Collen asked. "The sky is so dark already."

"We will know well enough, Master Collen." Man Lyr rode up on his Windhoove mount, Fierceheart. Kara Falcon perched on his shoulder.

"Little Dragon?"

Rhyan met his gaze. "I am ready."

"Kara will remain to aid you in the battle." He nodded toward Morgan and Ailem. "Our Windhooves will return once they have carried us to the mouth of the tunnel. They are not suited to the underground passages beneath the Tor."

"My grandfather, sir, bade me to protect and follow the Lady Rhyan, and that's what I mean to do." Collen's brown eyes fixed on Rhyan's face as he spoke.

She said nothing. The Eyestone had begun to grow warm against her chest. A new thrumming, like the buzzing of bees, tingled in her fingers.

Let the power come.

"I understand," Man Lyr said. "See then that you remain behind us within the tunnel, Collen William's son. But know that neither you nor I will be able to enter the center of the labyrinth and face Druin. That is for the Chosen alone."

Tura reached her hand out to Rhyan. "I am not to go with you, Chosen. I have pledged to keep these beasts at bay while you face the true enemy. My heart, however, shall hold you safe. I have seen the power you bear in the Eyestone. I believe in the wisdom of the Kirrin. You shall prevail."

Yes. Rhyan breathed deep. *I have the power, but I am in control. I am...still myself.*

"Thank you, daughter of Alder." She touched the upturned palm of the Faerie warrior. "Your faith gives me strength. Have you seen my cousin?"

Tura shook her head. "Nor have I seen Fiona Wyddandaughter. No doubt they have placed themselves in the fighting units best suited to their abilities."

"No doubt." But Rhyan wasn't as certain. *Was Hale still loyal to his father?* Her gaze slid to where Man Lyr waited. *And what of Fiona? Had she spoken to her father? What was the truth of Elina's death?*

"You are our only hope, Rhyan Kember." In preparation for the battle, Kel Dana's cheeks now bore the white sunburst symbol. "May your path be even and your heart strong."

"I will not forget Dun na Riogh," Rhyan said.

"Nor will I." Kel Dana bowed.

Morgan moved his mount closer and took Rhyan's hand. "I wish that our paths lay together, my friend. But I must fight and lead my men. We will hold the Dreadspawn at bay, Rhyannon Kember, I give my word. Keep safe and do what must be done."

"Yes, keep safe." Ailem did not offer his hand but held her gaze with his own. "As leader of my people, I must also take part in the battle." *'My heart goes with you. We still need to talk. I am yours, my Chosen.'*

"Ailem, I—"

A sudden piercing keen rose above the wind. Kara Falcon took wing as Morgan's horse reared and twisted, its eyes wild. The Windhooves moved to calm him.

"What's happening?" Rhyan shouted to make herself heard above the terrible howling.

Man Lyr motioned toward the flatlands below.

A gray-green vent opened in the black fog, and the terrors described by Broch Fraser emerged from the unnatural cloud. Skeleton-like wraith-generals mounted on red griffins called out orders to harpies and fang-bears, while hundreds of unnatural beasts walked forward on two legs, howling and screeching their battle cries. The Dreadspawn moved into well-formed ranks that covered Windover Plain.

Rhyan clenched her hands into tight fists.

"Stones and bones! What are those one-eyed creatures?" Collen pointed to a score or more of huge, ferocious warriors carrying great spiked clubs.

"They are Balor—cave dwellers from the North Islands," Man Lyr answered.

"Those look to be men of Valles!" Morgan directed their attention to the left flank. "Why are they fighting alongside the Dreadspawn?"

Man Lyr shook his head. "They are Death Warriors—the cursed soul-stealing shape-shifters that take on the likeness and capture the memories of the last living thing they killed."

"And where is our friend, the Dark Knight, I wonder?" Morgan asked.

"There!" Tura pointed to the standard of the red dragon on a midnight field. The flag flapped and snapped as its bearer marched through the parted ranks of the Dreadspawn armies, heralding the arrival of his master: The Dark Knight of Cumbria.

As if he felt Rhyan's gaze, the Knight's voice reached out

once more.

'You needlessly risk the lives of those about you, dragon-child. Even if you save your sister, you will lose others in the battle. Why not join us? Deliver my master the Eyestone. He and I will depart this land and leave you to rule. Is this not what you desire? A throne and those you love safe about you? Join us!'

"Little Dragon, we must hurry," Man Lyr said. "It is time."

If I accept the offer, am I powerful enough to force Druin to keep his bargain?

A horn sounded and the Dalrians charged down the hill toward the Dreadspawn. The Faerie, the Plainspeople, and the men of Valles thundered a few heartbeats behind. Everything depended on the allies pushing back the Dreadspawn enough to allow Rhyan to enter the hidden tunnel entrance and descend to the caves beneath the Tor.

Rhyan, Man Lyr, and Collen rode across the racing tide of warriors to take the proper position. It felt like a wild and violent dance, with the army running and riding around them. Finally, the trio reached the shadow of the tumbled boulders, where they would wait for their path to open.

The position also provided a clear view of the battle. Rhyan's heart raced as Tura thrust her blade into the heart of a ravening bear-man leaping toward her Windhoove mount.

A chorus of howls pulled her attention left. She narrowed her eyes and peered through the haze. The same black wolves that had attacked the companions at the River Briden now surrounded Dougal Fraser and a handful of his kinsmen.

Tura turned in that direction. *"Eadarowan!"* the Faerie woman yelled. She charged toward the Fraser.

A black arrow flew swift and sure and struck her full in the chest.

"No!" Rhyan moaned. Her gaze followed the path of the arrow back to the bowman. The Dark Knight of Cumbria, arrayed in gleaming black battle armor, raised the visor of his helmet. His glittering eyes, clearly visible even from such a distance, fixed on her in triumph.

With a surge of anger, she laid her hand on the Eyestone.

"No," Man Lyr said. "Do not give in, Little Dragon! Your task lies elsewhere."

She gritted her teeth and tried to swallow the heat and fury within.

Morgan raised the starred silver sword of his ancestors. He spurred his warhorse through the hot, choking wind toward the evil knight.

Loud shouts and screams drew Rhyan's attention to a skirmish just below their hiding place. What appeared to be Fairie, Dalrians, and men of the Southland fought against the Plainspeople. With horror, she realized that the Kanesga battled Death Warriors. Kel Dana fired arrow after arrow, striking down many of the loathsome beings. But she stopped and lowered her bow when a Plainswarrior stepped forward to fight, a white sunburst tattoo clearly visible on his arm.

Her brother.

Kel Dana stood as if frozen, staring at the Death Warrior.

"It isn't him!" Rhyan shouted. "It's an evil trick."

Suddenly, Kara Falcon dived down from the smoky, shadowed sky and dug her long talons into the Death Warrior's face. The creature screamed and grabbed Kara, flinging her to the ground.

The falcon had broken the spell.

"Fire!" Kel Dana screamed. The arrows hummed past her.

Where is Ailem? Rhyan scanned the field. She could not see him.

'Be strong, Rhyan. Be true.'

"There!" Man Lyr pointed at the now-visible tunnel entrance.

They'd done it. But at what cost?

Rhyan urged Starlight toward the blackened trees that marked the entrance. As they rode past the dead evergreens, she remembered the pine needles beneath the tree where she had hidden during that last game in the woods with Elspeth. And the vision she'd had.

A dark-armored hunter with black bow in hand.

He nocks a red-fletched arrow and points it toward the heart of the sleeping deer.

Am I the deer...or the hunter?

'*Chosen,*' Starlight's mind-voice shocked Rhyan into awareness.

'*Chosen,*' the Windhoove repeated, '*we cannot go on. This way was not meant for Windhoove kind. Even if the walls would accommodate us, the pressing in of the earth would lead to madness. You must dismount and allow us to wait for you here at the entrance.*'

Man Lyr stood at Starlight's flank. He and Collen had already left their mounts.

Rhyan stared at her old mentor as his long-fingered hand reached out to take hers.

Was he good or evil? Did he speak the truth or lie?

"Come now, Rhyan, the time is almost upon us."

Fire thrummed in her veins.

Am I good or evil? Will I betray my friends to save my sister?

She took the wizard's hand and dismounted.

Farewell, Starlight.

'*Farewell, Chosen.*'

Man Lyr led the way, carrying a lighted torch. Rhyan followed and Collen brought up the rear. The stone passage plunged downward, deep into the Tor. Rhyan kept one hand on the wall as they descended through the twists and turns of the tunnel.

Once, muffled echoes of the battle above reached her ears, but soon she heard only the scraping and shuffling of hurried steps and labored breaths.

As they continued, a pulsing glow grew in the distant darkness of the tunnel. Around a long curve, they came upon a vaulted cavern. In the center of the vast space stood a gate crafted of a dark metal. Large, white, glowing stones adorned each post—moonstones that matched the Eyestone.

The entrance to the labyrinth.

A rush of heat! Fire in the center of her chest! Rhyan walked past Man Lyr toward the labyrinth gate. She lifted the Eyestone's chain and pulled the talisman from beneath her shirt. The white stone now twinkled a deep violet at its molten center.

"Remember, hold the stone! Keep it—" Man Lyr choked on the words. He clutched at his throat, and then fell to the cavern floor, helpless.

Collen rushed back and knelt beside the wizard.

A strange curtain fell between Rhyan and her companions, like a veil of liquid glass. Collen stood and tried to move back toward her, only to be blocked by the invisible barrier. His lips moved, but she heard nothing but her own ragged breath and the beating of her heart.

"Do you wish to enter?" A rich, kind voice fell into the silence like a large pebble dropped into a deep well.

Rhyan turned. A tall figure stood near the gate, hooded and cloaked in dark red fabric.

"I am the Gate Warden. Do you wish to enter the first circuit?" His words echoed.

Man Lyr said nothing of a Gate Warden.

Collen and the fallen wizard could not help her now.

This choice is mine.

"I do," she whispered.

The metal gate swung open of its own accord and Rhyan entered. As she passed between the lintel posts, the moonstones flashed a violet surge of light. She gripped the Eyestone tightly and followed the Gate Warden into the labyrinth.

TWENTY-THREE
The Labyrinth

Rhyan stood on a stool in the center of a large room. A group of women surrounded her, talking and laughing as they tucked and arranged her billowing amethyst skirts. The room had no windows. She could not tell if it was day or night. A roaring fire burned in the hearth, blasting heat and casting deep purple flame-light amidst the ebon shadows dancing on the stone walls.

Where am I? What is happening?

"We can't have Lady Rhyan catching her death, now can we?" Nanny Bess said.

"But I'm so hot." Sweat rolled down her back.

"Nonsense!" Nanny clucked as she pulled the laces of Rhyan's plum-dark bodice tighter and tighter.

"I can hardly breathe!" She squirmed out of Nanny's grasp.

Hale laughed from the corner of the room. "Now you look like a true court lady, my fair cousin."

"I don't want to be a court lady!"

"That will be your role now, sister." At the door of their bedroom, Elspeth pulled on long, dark leather gloves. She wore a tight matching tunic and pants, and her golden hair, arranged in a battle braid, shone glossy and beautiful in the purple firelight.

"But Elspeth, I'm the one who is different. I'm not made for an ordinary life!"

Heat pulsed in Rhyan's blood, moving through her veins like broken glass. She moaned.

"Put down the Eyestone," the Gate Warden whispered. "It is the cause of this pain. You are not meant to travel the labyrinth path with such powerful magic."

Rhyan shook her head. *Man Lyr told me to hold the stone. I must keep it.*

The amethyst glow deepened to an inky cobalt mist as the room, the women, Nanny, Hale, and Elspeth slowly dissolved in the haze.

Rhyan took a step and passed the second gate.

She found herself in the Hall of Mirrors at Rath Mormar. The dancers from her earlier vision stood frozen around her, their silver garments now silky midnight cerulean.

"Help me!" Rhyan stumbled toward Morgan, who watched from the dais.

"Of course, my beautiful lady," he said.

"Too hot..." Rhyan cringed against the pain. She reached to grasp the Eyestone.

"Stop!" Ailem strode forward, drawing his sword. The silver emeralds on the blade had turned to tanzanite. "She belongs to me! She is my love."

My love, my love. Desire thrummed in Rhyan's breast. She closed her eyes and imagined his breath, cool and soothing in the hollow of her neck.

"I understand your craving—your desire, Faerie lord, but I cannot concede." Morgan drew his own blade. "I covet the same."

Morgan loves me, too?

She envisioned a throne next to the Steward's. She sat beside him as partner. Together they dispensed justice, and when alone, his arms slid around her.

The heat intensified...indigo coals bursting into flame...her heart engulfed. "I'm dying, help me."

"The Eyestone," the Gate Warden whispered. "It causes the pain...lay down this burden."

"I did not ask to feel this! I did not ask to be loved!" Rhyan cried out.

A glaring sapphire light flashed as she passed the third gate.

She stood in the Watchguard practice yard at Caer Kember.

"Raise your weapon!" Tura brandished her sword in Rhyan's face. "How can you learn to fight if you will not raise your weapon?"

"I...don't have a sword."

"Liar! You have a mighty weapon. You should be able to strike me down. You should defeat our enemy. But you refuse to use your power!" Tura threw down her sword. "You disgust me, Chosen. Your weakness sickens me."

"I can use it!" Rhyan yelled. "I saved the children at Dun na Riogh."

"Show me then, weakling!"

Sky blue lightning shot from the Eyestone destroying Tura in an azure mist.

"No," Rhyan whispered.

What have I done?

She fell to the ground, chest heaving, lungs filled with knives.

"The stone is corrupt, Chosen," the Gate Warden soothed. "Those who sent you here lied to you. Lay it down."

Waving him away, Rhyan dragged herself upright and continued through the fourth gate, emerging amid the tall swaying grass of the Plains.

"Have you come to mourn with me, Chosen?"

Kel Dana knelt before her, cradling the dead body of her brother. "You are powerful, indeed, Rhyan Kember." Tears fell from the Plainswoman's glistening emerald eyes. "Yes, you saved the children, but you could not save Mostfa, the only family I had left."

"I'm sorry I wasn't in time..." Rhyan said. "I don't want to be the Chosen. Let me go back..."

"Peace," the Gate Warden soothed. "Lay down the Eyestone and, even now, you will win out. Your old place awaits...home awaits..."

No, I must keep going. I must reach the center with the stone in hand.

The fifth gate swung open.

Rhyan woke and sat up in her bed. Thank goodness! Wait...it was like her room, but...the coverlet was embroidered with yellow blossoms, not brown. And strange golden leaves lined the walls. She looked across the room at Elspeth's bed.

Empty!

Rhyan threw back the covers and ran barefoot to the door. Man Lyr waited in the corridor, his gray cloak replaced by a tarnished amber robe.

"Yes, I lied to you, Rhyan Kember. Sadly, you were too weak and ignorant to notice. I strive for my own redemption and care not for the fate of one girl. Your sister is lost—but for a worthy cause."

"Man Lyr, no! I must save her!"

"I've admired your love for your sister...but, where is she? I think you, too, have forgotten her. You, like me, think only of your power...your fame."

"No! No, I haven't forgotten, I—"

"I thought you were special. Bound for great things. Was I mistaken?"

The sixth gate disintegrated in a brilliant sunset flash.

Ailem stood before her, surrounded by bushes covered in orange *alamathra.*

Rhyan reached out to touch one of the butterflies. The heat from her body ignited the insect, setting fire to the entire shrub. In seconds, all lay in a pile of ash at her feet.

"Ailem? Ailem, I'm sorry—help me!"

"When I first saw you, Rhyan, you were the most alive person I had ever met—lit from within by a bright candle flame of life. I loved you from that moment."

"Ailem, I loved you, too, but—"

"But you wished for power, Rhyan. You yearned for it—coveted it! But you could not see through the illusion, my love. Power will not bring you love. It will not make you wise, or bring peace to your land, or save your sister." He pointed to an arched doorway and Rhyan saw her sister's shape enter it and disappear.

"Elspeth?" Rhyan ran through the doorway and found herself in an abandoned Caer Kember, calling her sister's name over and over. She chased the echoes of her own voice and fought the heat that burned in her breast, trying to ignore the feeling that, like the *alamathra*, she might ignite and disintegrate into ash.

The Gate Warden waited at the door to the castle garden. "Free yourself. Give up the stone and all will be well."

Rhyan pushed him out of the way. She groped around her neck, found the Eyestone, and brought the hot, glowing stone up to the level of her eyes.

Then she stepped into the garden and the seventh gate—the red Dragon's Gate—swung open.

"Llud will help me," she whispered. She ran down the familiar pathway and found the old gardener bent down, pulling weeds from a hedge of scarlet roses.

"Llud?"

But it wasn't Llud. Collen—his skin wrinkled with age and tears streaming down his weary face—stood and turned to face her.

"The garden is dying." He held up a withered, burned plant.

"You left it. You ran away to glory and now they're dying—the garden, Grandad, Lord Angus, Lady Rose, everyone! You did not come home. You lied to me."

"You can return to them even now! You can still save them!" the Gate Warden shouted. "All will be as it was." He reached out his hand. "Give the Eyestone into my keeping and be free from this torment."

"I am sorry, so sorry," Rhyan cried.

A scream shattered the walls of the garden. Collen disappeared.

Rhyan stood on the edge of a great cliff looking down on racing rapids far below. The wreckage of a carriage lay scattered along the rocky riverbank.

"They left us," she whispered. "My sister and I have had to face this evil day alone. Better that we had all died together."

Fiona stood beside her. The Faerie woman wore Elspeth's favorite gown, but the fabric had changed to a dark, blood red and her hair had been braided with sharp-faceted rubies instead of pearls. Kara Falcon gripped Fiona's shoulder, the bird's blue eyes infected with red sores.

"My mother is dead," Fiona said. "He lied to me and then he killed her." She pointed across the divide toward a crimson-cloaked figure.

"Man Lyr?" But when the figure pulled back his hood, she saw Keven's face.

"Must I die for you again, Rhyan Kember? Solve the riddle, make the choice, take action." He ran to the edge of the cliff and jumped.

Rhyan closed her eyes against the pain. Loneliness and despair washed over her in a great wave. She sank to her knees.

No parents. No sister. Aunt Rose and Uncle Angus are gone. Nanny is gone. Keven is dead. Man Lyr? Ailem? Llud? Tears pricked her eyes. *At last I will cry...now that I have lost everything.*

"Of what use are they to you?" the Gate Warden asked. "They

lied to you. They left you. They have taken all and given nothing."

Uncle Angus and Aunt Rose did hide the truth from us, Rhyan thought. *Llud lied. Man Lyr lied to me about who he was and what he wanted from me. The Faerie drugged me. My parents left me...Elspeth left me...*

Keven left, but he died to save me, he chose me.

Collen is here, faithful.

And Ailem...?

Help me! Rhyan screamed in her mind. *Please, Ailem!*

'Be strong my friend, my love. Be strong.'

His words kissed her pain like a brief, cool breeze. A brief second of sweet reprieve.

"You are wrong, Gate Warden," she said, and opened her eyes.

Rhyan stood in a red-washed circle of light. Silence echoed around her. She still clasped the Eyestone.

I made it.

"Well done, *Chosen.*" The Gate Warden stepped into the circle. He removed his hood and shook out a length of long black hair, his bright-gold eyes like liquid metal.

Rhyan stared as his eyes grew larger and the wrinkles in his face deepened. His skin took on a florid, blood-scarlet color as he grew taller and taller. A great red-scaled tail slithered out behind him.

A dragon!

"Druin!" Rhyan breathed.

The dragon laughed. "Yesss, Chosen. I am Druin. Trapped within thisss labyrinth by a petty hedge wizard those many centuriesss ago. I have grown in ssstrength and power as I waited for the weaknesss of your bloodline to show itself.

"I am done with these gamesss," the beast hissed. "I had to play along to bring you to me. You are here now...at the center...within my trap. Give me the Eyestone and these worthlesss ones ssshall be free."

The dragon shifted. Across the cavern, beyond the misted veil, Collen helped Man Lyr to his feet.

"What about Elspeth?"

"Your sssister is a weak vessel," Druin said. "Your uncle's tactics have kept her sssubdued. I will free her from her wretchednesss once you give me the Eyestone."

She licked her dry, cracked lips. "My friends... Ailem, Collen..."

"My faithful knight will sssoon sssubdue them. Perhaps you will also aid me, Chosen? Join me now and forget these faithless ones! You can sssee the path before you—release yourself from this agony! Give me the Eyestone! Otherwise you will not sssurvive!"

"No," Rhyan whispered.

"Then you have utterly failed, Rhyannon Kember, for they will all die!"

"No!" She fell to her knees.

The dragon reared back and exhaled, striking Rhyan with a blast of flame.

TWENTY-FOUR

Two Silver, One Black

Ailem heard Rhyan call his name one last time before the mind-link was broken. He held the thought of her close as he turned back to the turmoil around him. His breath moved in and out of tired lungs in heavy, desperate gasps. He wiped a bloodied hand across his sweaty brow. Had it been only minutes since the battle began? Or hours? How long ago had he dismounted, sending a wounded Duskmane from the field? He could not tell. The moans of dying men and beasts echoed in the semi-darkness around him, but for one moment, he stood alone in a circle of calm on this field of death.

A flash of light caught his eye and the clash of two mighty swords shook the air.

"Dalria!" A fearless voice called.

Ailem ran toward the combatants. Sparks from their clashing weapons grew brighter, outlining their moving shapes against the smoke of the battle. Thrust and parry. Circle and feint. Morgan battled the Dark Knight of Cumbria.

The knight rushed forward, using his black-starred sword to

force the Steward's silver blade to the side. The evil knight then threw an armored shoulder into his opponent's chest, knocking him to the ground.

"*Eadarowan!*" Ailem raised the starred sword of Havenhome and ran forward. He must stop the knight from delivering the killing blow! He must save Morgan!

But the Dark Knight turned his back on the Steward and walked away.

Why?

As Morgan struggled to rise, a shadow moved closer. The flash of a blade rose high over the Steward's back.

"No!" Ailem pulled his own short knife and flung it toward the assailant. The man's death cry echoed as the weapon pierced his heart.

Ailem raced forward but slowed, and then froze in shock.

Morgan turned and cradled the head of the man who had just attempted to kill him.

Garth macNeill stared, sightless, into the shadowed sky.

"Steward...your pardon, he—"

"I know," Morgan whispered, closing his uncle's eyes. "I know, my friend. No pardon is necessary, but I...I must still mourn his passing. He was not always my enemy."

"How touching." The Dark Knight sneered, turning back toward them. "Don't fool yourself, Steward. He hated you. How eagerly he sent his man to collect the spirit of Bridelyn from the River Wenden when I seeded the idea in his traitorous mind. How much his hatred festered when—after unleashing her wrath into the River Eiren—you did not die by Bridelyn's magic at the Ford. From leagues away, I felt his hatred burning and boiling within his diseased heart. When I called to him across the field, '*Come and kill,*' how joyfully he answered—eager to see you die, Steward."

The evil knight roared laughter. "But, he was weak and now I must finish the task."

As Ailem helped Morgan to his feet, their two swords—one

bearing the white emeralds of Havenhome and the other the etched starbursts of Dalria—swung upward in a single motion.

"There are two of us now, Evil One," the Faerie said.

"Can I not squash two insects with my boot as easily as one? My master has made me powerful, Faerie-prince." With one hand, he swung the black-starred broadsword from side to side. "In a few moments, once he is freed from bondage, my power will grow ten-fold. It is a pity that I will kill you now and you will not be here to witness our final triumph. What feasting there will be! I hear the flesh of Windhooves makes a tasty roast."

No. No. No! Ailem closed his eyes and saw a broken, sorrowful young girl lying motionless on a cave floor. A mighty dragon stood over her.

Do not let this happen, Rhyan! Be strong. Remember, you are the Chosen!

TWENTY-FIVE

Center

Druin Canwyr had disappeared. A young woman stood in the dragon-lord's place.

"What happened?" Rhyan asked.

"You have reached the true center of the labyrinth." The woman's hair shimmered red to gold to black to brown to silver-white as she moved toward Rhyan. "You have passed the seven gates and faced the crisis. Where you go from here is your own choice."

"But...the fire. Am I dead?"

"In a way, yes, you have died. Your self that was...is no longer. Through the power of the Eyestone, you have faced all and lost everything. You have become both what you wished...and what you feared. Now you must choose."

"What should I do?"

"You must either give up the Eyestone to Druin or keep the power for yourself. You must choose well and quickly, for the time of the moondark is upon us."

"I must keep it," Rhyan said. "It was given to me by the

Kirrin. Only I can wield it. Man Lyr told me to hold it." She closed her eyes as the memory of the stone's potent energy washed over her. "How will I defeat Druin otherwise? I need the Eyestone."

The woman took Rhyan's hand and ran her fingers lightly over the labyrinth ring of Mirandrabeth. "Do not grasp the outward signs of power too tightly, Rhyannon Kember. The North Queen did so to her everlasting sorrow."

Rhyan remembered Mirandrabeth's words: *Do not, in your pride, turn from the path of the Goddess.*

"Look within once more, Chosen. Seek the truth. Every journey in life is like traveling to the center of this prismed labyrinth and then making your way back." Slender fingers touched Rhyan's cheek. "Throughout the journey here to face Druin, you have recognized your fears and failings. Now is the time to accept them. Truth—that is what gives you power. Not any talisman you hold, nor the latent magic of your bloodline, nor the hidden part of you that Druin planted. Here at the center, you have won the power of choice, Rhyannon Kember."

"I don't understand." She felt as if she teetered, alone, on the edge of a great abyss.

"The answer lies within." The woman smiled, and her hair flashed from red to gold. It stirred a forgotten memory in Rhyan's heart.

"Are you my mother?" Rhyan grasped the question like a rope.

"I am the mother of all," the woman answered. "I am the devotion of your Nanny and the kindness of Rose Kember. I am the beauty of Elspeth and the lost sweetness of your mother, Branwen. I am the strength of Tura of Alder and the steadfast honor of Kel Dana of the Plains. I am the wisdom of the Lady Sianne and the anger of Bridelyn. I am the loyalty of the dowager Lady Steward of Dalria, the pride of Mirandrabeth, and the love of lost Lysana. I am the wild storm that cleansed Eldon Wood and the soft summer breeze in Old Llud's garden. I am the darkness and light inside you, *duonin* Rhyannon Kember. More ancient than any wizard. Stronger than any warrior. Wiser than any queen. I am Goddess! I am truth!"

A bright white bolt of lightning tore from the granite ceiling and struck the ground at Rhyan's feet. She collapsed.

When she opened her eyes, the Goddess was no longer with her.

"Where have you been, Chosssen?" Druin asked. Still in his terrible dragon form, he lay coiled like a snake on the floor of the cavern. His voice dripped with falsity. "You are powerful indeed if my fire did not harm you. You are the true heir to my blood. These are weak vesselsss."

Rhyan's breath caught as he moved in a quick blur and transformed into human form once more. Laughing, he swung his hand toward the shadows beyond the labyrinth veil where Collen and Man Lyr—and now Fiona and Hale—stood still and silent.

"But you, my dear dragon-child, Man Lyr named you truly. Here is the secret that you have feared and longed to know. I have done more than just exert control over the feeble and worried heart of your princely grand-sire and the damaged mind of your uncle, Evnis. Over long years, beginning from the very moment of my imprisonment, I have conserved my weakened magic, biding my time until it became sufficient to my purpose. Then, in the darkness of night, I traveled the dream plane, visiting your mother in spirit form while she slept with a life—tiny and formless—in her womb. Using my hoarded magic, I spent it all to cross the veil and leave a drop of my own blood to simmer in her unborn child. I did not sense then that two souls rested there."

Bile rose in Rhyan's throat. *No, no, no!*

Druin laughed. "I see by the fear in your eyes that you now understand the burning in your veins. *You are the bearer of my blood!* I feel it—it pulses and flows within your body.

"I am maddened that I can also feel within you a power that

is not mine. I smell the stink of it on your spirit—a strain of the true ancient magic. The cankerous purity of that magic has foiled my plans, given you control over this prison of a labyrinth, and let you hold the ancient Eyestone. The power your weak mother inherited—that of the cursed Goddess!

"Even now, your dragon-blood wars against the Goddess's putrid light! Turn away from her and join me, *daughter*. Join me and embrace your true self! Join me and save your sister."

Druin pointed and an area of shadows cleared just beyond the boundary of the labyrinth. Elspeth lay motionless on the floor of the cavern. Prince Evnis of Windover knelt beside her. He held a long knife in his shaking hand.

"No!" Rhyan cried.

"She is only asleep, dragon-child. You can save her! Give me the Eyestone! It will allow me to leave this labyrinth without spilling your sister's blood. Once I am free, you will rule this land unquestioned and you shall have *all* that you desire.

"Otherwise..."

Rhyan stared at the evil dragon wizard. His long, dark hair, streaked with red and silver, hung lank around a ragged, but perhaps once-handsome face. His eyes glowed. His golden-amber eyes.

Golden-eyed dragon-child...

He is part of me, but not all of me.

Druin smiled. "Otherwise, I shall have to ask your uncle to speed your sister on her journey. Once her life's blood is spilled over this gate, I will be free! If you deny me the Eyestone, then I have no choice. Evnis?"

Drool spilled from between the Prince of Windover's lips, pooling on Elspeth's motionless arm. He raised the knife over his niece's heart.

"No!" Hale ran forward, drawing his weapon.

Evnis whirled and lunged at his son. He stumbled and slashed the long knife across his son's leg. Hale cried out and nearly dropped his sword. The prince scrambled to his feet and thrust the knife again, but this time his son stood ready. Hale swung his sword and struck his father just under the arm. Rhyan gasped as the prince collapsed to the ground, his wound gushing blood.

Too much blood.

"Father?" Hale's weapon clattered on the stone.

"Useless fool!" Druin spat. "Perhaps the son will be a better tool. Poor young Hale who thought to sneak down through the dungeons of Windover Tor and rescue his cousins. Pick up your weapon, new Prince of Windover." He raised a hand and Hale jerked and started as if a puppeteer pulled his strings.

"No!" But even as he protested, Hale bent and reached for his sword with a shaking hand.

"I will not allow it." Man Lyr stepped forward.

Druin laughed. "You are not the famed White Wizard of old, Mannawyddan. *Great heart*? You could not save your beloved from me, even then. A woman who loves is always weak. All I had to do was threaten you, and she sacrificed herself."

"Do not demean her selflessness, Druin. Elina trapped you within the labyrinth. She defeated you."

"What heroism! I can still taste the sound of her screams as she burned in my fire."

"You will pay for her death, Evil One," Fiona yelled.

A horrible laugh escaped Druin's lips. He raised his arms and sent a hot burst of lightning toward Fiona, but before the deadly bolt struck, Man Lyr threw his body in front of his daughter. The jagged line of crackling fire struck the gray-robed wizard and he fell to the floor of the cavern like a rag doll.

"No!" Fiona stared, shocked and unbelieving, at her father's body.

"Must this game continue, dragon-child? Give me the Eye-stone or I will have the Wyddandaughter pick up the knife. She will shed your sister's blood and free me. Do you want to lose her as you lost your weak and trusting parents? You do know that I sent my dark servant to pursue their carriage on the

Whyte Clyff Road? My power was still too weak for me to do the deed myself. Such a tragic accident."

He killed my parents.

Rhyan slowly inhaled and exhaled. She lifted the Eyestone and gazed into its gleaming opalescent light. At the swirling center of the stone, the Goddess stood with arms outstretched and eyes closed.

'Choose, my daughter.'

'Do not turn from the path of the Goddess,' said Mirandrabeth.

'When the time comes,' said the Kirrin, *'you will know. Surrender yourself to the truth. Let go.'*

'The Eyestone is the key,' said the Eldest.

Bridelyn's vision showed the Eyestone piercing the soul of its bearer and revealing...

'Truth—that is what gives you power,' said the Goddess.

'I love you, Rhyan,' whispered Ailem.

'I trust you,' said Collen. *'I will always trust you.'*

Finally, she saw her own reflection in the Eyestone. She saw the woman whose face had appeared in the whitewood Gate of *Eadarowan.* The *duonin*, light and dark, powerful, strong, and...

True.

A cold, clean fire burned in the center of her chest. She felt no pain now, only clarity. The vision in the Bridemere had come to pass. She lifted the chain bearing the Eyestone over her head.

"Cousin, what are you doing?" Hale yelled.

Collen met her eyes and nodded as she handed the glowing Eyestone to Druin.

"No, Chosen, no!" Fiona wept over her father's lifeless body.

The evil wizard threw back his head and laughed. He clutched the Eyestone to his chest and stepped through the Dragon's Gate.

His laughter dissolved into screams. He writhed in pain even as he clutched the Eyestone tighter in his frantic hands.

Inside Rhyan, wintry fire continued to grow.

"Aaaaghh!" the sorcerer screamed. "What trickery is this?"

Druin staggered about the cavern. He tried to discard the talisman, but it would not leave his hand. He called forth his fire-magic to melt the Eyestone. It blistered and charred his own hands, but still the talisman remained. Screaming, he conjured an icy river to break through from the depth of the earth and wash away the burning pain of his mind and body. But the torrent of frigid water simply evaporated in a thick mist as it touched his skin and gave him no release.

Finally, he changed back into his dragon form.

In response, Rhyan freed the searing, icy fire within herself. She moaned at the pain, but closed her eyes, reveling in the tearing exhilaration of it.

What is happening?

Yet, even as she asked the question, she knew the answer. She would not take a deer's shape, she thought, remembering her long-ago wish under the tree in Eldon Wood. Not a gentle forest animal, but a beast of strength and power.

I am Plendraig...child of the dragon!

White-ice flames licked their way throughout her body until the very tips of her fingers felt full of frozen fire. Her neck stretched, and her legs lengthened. A ripple of sharp pain spread over the surface of her skin as prism-white scales formed over her new, muscular, reptilian shape.

I am a dragon-child.

Druin roared. Lunging through the thick fog, he breathed red flame at Rhyan.

Her golden-faceted dragon eyes closed against the heat.

He cannot hurt me.

She reached out her dragon talon and took the Eyestone from her enemy. The stone's glow warmed Rhyan even through her scaled skin. Her mind contracted and then expanded in an explosion of awareness. Scenes flicked across her consciousness, almost too quickly for her to comprehend.

Druin as a young boy. Starving and sickly, he poured a flask of black powder into a cauldron of stew.

Then, older, setting fire to an animal in a cage.

As a man, holding a bloody knife over the still form of a child.

The visions raced away, lost in white flashes of power as the Eyestone sank beneath her skin, melding with her dragon blood.

Rhyan-dragon faced her enemy without fear. With one slow breath, she filled her enormous lungs.

Crazed and roaring, Druin lashed out at her with his tail, but Rhyan barely felt the blow. She focused all her power and breathed her own terrible white fire, engulfing Druin in acid-opal flames.

"Curssse you, Rhyan Kember!" The dragon-lord screamed and then fell silent.

Rhyan's dragon eyes watched Druin's spirit disperse into the stones of the labyrinth floor.

"It is done."

Rhyan turned and faced the Goddess, bright and rainbow-gilt, standing again at the center of the labyrinth.

"What happened?"

"Did you forget that the labyrinth and the Eyestone are my weapons, child? The Eyestone gave Druin the power to pass through the Dragon's Gate, extinguishing the blood magic. But Druin was still subject to the true power of this labyrinth. He thought the labyrinth only contemplative, showing scenes and pictures as travelers walked the circuits to the center. He did not know that the journey *out* of the labyrinth is where the transformation occurs. It forces travelers to face and accept the fears and weaknesses and wrongs that they have done. For someone like Druin, the errors of his past were like a hundred sharp needles piercing his soul."

Rhyan nodded, remembering the visions she had seen when she took the Eyestone back from Druin.

"But how will I get out? Am I trapped here? If I leave, will I go mad, too?"

"The Eyestone is in your blood now," the Goddess said. "You

are free to exit the labyrinth. But to do so, you must accept what Druin could not."

"Rhyan! Hear me!" Collen shouted from beyond the Dragon's Gate. "The water is rising...stone from the ceiling is falling..."

As Rhyan stepped back through the seventh gate, the Goddess, the Lady of the Labyrinth faded in a deep ruby haze of color. She smiled a farewell and left one last message in Rhyan's mind.

'*Be brave, daughter. Be true...*'

RED.

Fiona Wyddandaughter stood crying on the bank of the River Briden, clasping a bloody cloak to her breast.

Those who love face difficult choices, Fiona. We cannot judge the hearts of others when we have not walked their path. We are not shaped by those who have lied to us or left us, but by the truths we accept and the actions we take.

Keven of Tralleigh stood across the river. His scarlet cloak billowed in a phantom breeze. He smiled and tipped his hat at Rhyan.

Yes, Keven, I chose to act. I chose to give away power and to embrace it. And I held on to myself. Thank you for your story and your sacrifice.

The spirits of Rhyan's parents floated peacefully in the ochre-washed mist of the river's rapids. Branwen's lips moved. '*We love you, daughter. We are proud of you. Take care of your sister...*'

I will. Rhyan turned from the riverbank to enter the garden at Caer Kember.

Collen knelt amid the scarlet blooms.

I am changed, Collen, but I will be faithful to those in my care. I will return. I will earn your trust and friendship.

ORANGE.

Ailem stood before her holding a single sunset-flamed candle. His sad eyes reproached her.

I have craved power, Ailem. And now that I hold it, I know all too well its dangers. I am not perfect—nor would I ever want to be so. My power is part of who I am. I cannot reject it, just as I cannot reject my feelings for you. I ask you to accept me for who I am...

Ailem blew out the candle and a string snapped against Rhyan's heart.

YELLOW.

The gold-leafed bedroom once again materialized around her. But this time, Elspeth slept there, her blonde hair spread like a fan across her pillow.

Thank the Goddess you are safe now, sister.

Man Lyr stood at the window gazing at Windover Tor. His form outlined in bright, bright sunlight.

I thank you, Man Lyr, for being the first to understand my restless desire to rise above the ordinary. I am grateful for all that you taught me. And I am sad that I will no longer have your counsel and wisdom. I know that the choices you made were those you thought best at the time. We must each come to the truth of who we are in our own way.

The old wizard turned to face Rhyan. Tears streamed down his lined face.

'You have grown, Little Dragon—in power and in wisdom. Both will serve you well in the challenges to come. Farewell.'

GREEN.

Kel Dana knelt amid the long grass near her fallen brother.

I am sorry that I did not come fully into my power in time to save Kai Mostfa. One life lost is one too many. I will never forget the dead of Dun na Riogh or any who died in the defeat of Druin.

The Plainswarrior nodded, her emerald eyes filled with tears.

BLUE.

Tura lay motionless on the ground, the Dark Knight's arrow lodged in her heart.

Your bravery and loyalty will live forever, First Daughter of Alder. You were the first to show me that a woman can be a warrior. Every day of my life, I will honor you by living that truth with strength and courage.

Tura's spirit rose from her body, raising a translucent hand in farewell before dissolving in the sapphire haze of the smoky battlefield.

INDIGO.

Morgan of Dalria sat silent in the Hall of Mirrors at Rath Mormar. He motioned to the empty throne at his side, his inky blue eyes meeting Rhyan's.

There are many kinds of love, Morgan. For so long, I defined my-self by articulating what I was not. Your gentle and honorable words and actions helped me to better know what I am and what I can be. And your actions as Steward have given me something to strive for—a model for true wisdom and leadership. But I will not sit beside you, dear Morgan.

He bowed his head and the empty throne vanished.

VIOLET.

Nanny Bess wept over the midnight plum gown discarded on the floor at her feet.

Rhyan reached out to comfort her. *I know that you have made it your life's work to bring me up as a proper lady, Nanny. But I must follow my own path.*

As the old woman turned her head to look at Rhyan, Hale suddenly appeared in her place. He held a bloody purple sword and his father's body lay at his feet on the rock floor of the labyrinth.

My heart aches for you, Hale. You paid a terrible price to save my sister. I am sorry for my lack of trust and my constant question-ing of your honor. I judged without understanding. I was so wrong. You have proved your blood true, cousin. Noble and true. Thank you.

As she stepped through the final gate, Rhyan's dragon-power subsided and the labyrinth veil lifted. She held out her hands and stared at the human shape of them.

I am myself again—almost. The Eyestone had disappeared, but its swirling rainbow of colors pulsed beneath the white scales now covering her right hand and arm.

"Thank the Goddess!" Collen ran toward her. "We must escape!" He pointed to where Hale and Fiona struggled to help Elspeth out of the cave.

She allowed Collen to lead her forward. Looking back only once, she saw the water rise over the black scar on the stone where Druin had died in her fire. And, finally, the flood of water covered the gray-cloaked figure of Man Lyr.

TWENTY–SIX

The Price of Power

So many.

Rhyan stood alone, looking out over the desolation of Windover Plain. A bell tolled in the distance as uninjured survivors dug burial pits along the base of the Tor. The great mound itself would serve as a monument for those who had given their lives in the battle with the Dreadspawn.

And as a tomb for Man Lyr.

"I will bear this weight for all my long years," Fiona Wyddandaughter said before she left. "I go now to grieve alone and do what I can to redeem myself."

Tears pricked Rhyan's eyes. *Man Lyr! I am so sorry for thinking ill of you.*

'Chosen?' Starlight nudged her. *'Do not over-sorrow. The White Wizard set out on his path long ago...and the Wyddandaughter just begins hers. Kara Falcon will follow and see that she comes to no harm.'*

Rhyan laid her hand on his neck. *Thank you.*

As she climbed onto the Windhoove's back, Kel Dana rode

up the hill. Fresh black symbols of mourning had replaced the Plainswoman's yellow sunburst battle paint. Her eyes met Rhyan's.

Oh no.

"Chosen, I must tell you that Tura of Alder and Lord Angus Kember were both lost."

Rhyan's vision narrowed. She watched a lone gray feather float gently over the hillside, carried on the after-wind of the battle. The slow, hot hurt of grief's knife twisted in her heart.

She'd seen Tura's death, but Uncle Angus? She tried to remember the last time they had spoken. Had she said something cruel? Now she would never see him again.

I am sorry.

"I know not the ways of your people. Chosen," Kel Dana said. "But I would help you to mourn."

"My uncle should be buried at Kember." *Poor Aunt Rose!*

"I will make arrangements to transport his body," Kel Dana said.

"I must write a message to...to both my aunts. My cousin will want to write to his mother, as well." Rhyan touched her own cheek. "And could I—I mean, would you help me honor the dead as you have?"

Kel Dana placed a hand over her heart. "It would be my great privilege, Chosen." She pulled a small pouch from her tunic. "We have lost many this day and we shall both bear symbols proclaiming their noble sacrifice."

"The others, our...friends, were they injured?" Rhyan allowed the Plainswoman to paint her cheeks with firm strokes.

"Dougal Fraser took an arrow to the leg, but the healers say he will recover. Morgan macNeill is unharmed, though his uncle turned during the battle and Ailem Suir was forced to kill the traitor. The Steward and First Son together defeated the Dark Knight of Cumbria, but Ailem Suir was slashed in the face by the knight's black blade."

'Chosen, Duskmane brings the First Son with news of your sister.'

As he approached, Rhyan tried not to stare at the jagged scar running from Ailem's ear to his chin. Someone had stitched it and dressed it with a garish green ointment.

She wanted to reach out and comfort him, but she held back. They could never again be together. Fiona and the Eldest had both spoken of the Faerie abhorrence of transformation. But it was what Ailem had said of Druin that echoed in her mind now: *He is both man and dragon—a distortion of nature to be abhorred by all!*

Rhyan tugged her right sleeve down to cover her white-scaled arm.

Once he knows the truth he will hate me.

Ailem reached out with his mind-voice, but she blocked the link. His eyes met hers. He raised his eyebrows.

She looked away. Beneath her sleeve, the pearly scales of her arm pulsed in time with her heartbeat.

I am a dragon-child. I bear the blood of evil.

"Your sister wakens, Rhyan." Ailem spoke aloud. "May I talk to you after you have seen her?"

"Of course." She avoided his eyes and Starlight galloped her back to the healers' camp.

Morgan met her just outside the tent where Elspeth had lain unmoving since their return.

"Chosen, your sister has been through much. The healer says we must not tire or upset her in any way."

Rhyan nodded, then stepped into the dimly lit space.

"Elspeth?"

Her sister's wasted body shifted beneath a light blanket and her pale lids fluttered open. Blue eyes met amber. "Rhyan? Is it you? I've had strange dreams."

"Oh, Elspeth...I am so sorry! When I think of what—"

"Don't." Elspeth interrupted. "I cannot bear to think of any of it. My head is filled with dread echoes...smoky shadows...fire!

Uncle Evnis?" She breathed the question in a whisper so weak that Rhyan almost didn't hear.

"Dead." Rhyan closed her eyes for a moment.

"He was sick." Elspeth's thin fingers picked at the blanket.

Rhyan caught the healer's signal from the corner of her eye. "Let us talk of this later. You are ill and tired. I do not wish—"

"Wait!" Elspeth sat up. "I remember...you were...you were a dragon! You changed into a MONSTER! A dragon—like the RED DRAGON! He hurt me...No! Oh no, oh no..." She covered her face with her hands and curled into a ball. Weeping and sobbing, she rocked back and forth.

Rhyan reached out to comfort her sister. The scales of her arm shone bright in the muted light of the tent.

"Don't touch me! You are evil! You are not my sister...not my sister...I am alone."

The healer forced Elspeth to swallow a sleeping draught.

"Has she no other wounds?" Rhyan asked.

The healer shook her head. "It is her mind that suffers."

If I cannot help her, what use is my power?

Rhyan thought of Queen Mirandrabeth and her daughter Lysana. She watched her sister's face until Elspeth fell into a drugged, but peaceful, sleep.

Is this the price of victory? Have I sacrificed my sister's sanity for the dragon's power?

When Rhyan asked about Dougal, the healer directed her to a tent nearby. As she approached, she heard raised voices. Inside, Collen and Kel Dana attempted to hold the injured Dalrian down on his cot. Ailem and Morgan watched, each with his arms crossed.

"I am fine!" Dougal pulled the bundle he held away from Collen's hand.

Coming closer, Rhyan saw that, in addition to his leg wound, the clansman's arms bore long scratches and small bite marks.

"You feel fine because of the infusion for pain that has been given to you." Ailem turned toward Morgan. "Now...about that beast—"

"Do not harm it!" Dougal said. "It is innocent. It came to me on the battlefield where I fell—"

"We will decide its fate, Fraser," Morgan said. "Now, let us see it."

As Dougal held out the small black bundle of fur, the animal raised its head and yawned, showing a tiny set of ferocious teeth.

Rhyan gasped and stepped back. A wolf cub—the spawn of the Windover wolves!

"It must be destroyed!" Morgan frowned.

"Without doubt." Ailem put a hand to his sword.

Kel Dana nodded her agreement.

"It is innocent, Chosen!" Dougal said. "It cannot help its parentage."

"No, it cannot," Hale of Windover said.

Rhyan hadn't noticed her cousin sitting silent on one of the other cots. He limped closer to stand over Dougal and scratch the cub behind its tiny black ears.

Snap! Snap! The tiny wolf's razor-sharp teeth nipped at his hand.

Collen's clear brown eyes caught and held Rhyan's gaze. She knew that he also wanted to save the beast.

'I too wish to spare the small creature.'

Starlight! It was just such a beast that wounded you.

'It was not this beast, Chosen.'

But Ailem said the wolves were true evil—unnatural abominations. If I go against him...

'Chosen, the wolf-child's mind is full of thoughts of hunger and thirst. I sense no evil in him.'

Rhyan's heart ached with a fresh pain. *Wolf-child?*

"My cousin is right. The past should be put behind us. It is a time of new beginnings."

Hale raised weary eyes. "Thank you."

Rhyan reached out and touched the wet nose of the wolf

pup.

Kel Dana gasped, staring down at the reptilian gleam of her clearly visible pearly-scaled hand.

"By the Crown!" Morgan said.

Rhyan's gaze flew to Ailem. He, too, stared at her hand. The lines of his jaw tightened and his eyes narrowed.

She took a deep breath and reached out to him with her mind-voice once more.

This is who I am, Ailem. Light and dark. Dragon and human. That is the truth.

His eyes flickered as he received her words, but the First Son of Faerie gave no answer.

Collen laid a comforting hand on her arm.

"We are all changed by this journey." Rhyan spoke aloud this time. "This is who I am. This is my truth."

The wolf pup nipped at Rhyan's fingers. She scratched behind his ear and he leaned his soft, furry head against her dragon-hand.

"I think I'll name him *Calon-fawr*."

About the Author

Born in Canada, Leanne Pankuch currently lives in the Hudson Valley. When she's not writing about girls and women who break the rules, she reads way too many books. She loves wandering, music, history, fairy tales, graveyards, trees, rocks, dogs, her pirate husband, and her fellowship/family.

Connect with Leanne at:
leannepankuch.com
Facebook and Twitter: @talelady
Instagram: leannepan_author

Acknowledgements

I am most indebted to my husband, Ray, who I am lucky enough to have as a friend, advocate, and champion on this journey. He is never too busy to leap into my world and heroically help me through the seemingly endless series of problems that my characters tend to create for themselves. And he always knows when it is time for a trip to the bookstore. Bless you, love.

I would also like to thank:

My children—Sean, Nick, and Melissa—who provide constant encouragement, but also helpful and insightful criticism (we all know the criticism part mostly refers to Nick aka "Kill your Elves").

My ever-faithful "writing buddy," Carmela Martino, for her sage advice and support.

Designer Kara DeMaio at theblueprintstudio.com for her creative collaboration and assistance in building the map of Rhyan's world.

My critique group, the SWLs, for their valuable feedback.

The SCBWI for so many things, but especially the IL chapter for welcoming me to my very first writers conference in Woodstock many years ago. At the open mic, I read what would someday become the first chapter of *Dragon's Truth*. I still have the small slips of paper with the written feedback I received that night: *I want to read more! Great imagery—great voice! I'm already in your world. Can't wait to read the book!* Your words helped me to truly believe in myself as a writer.

The rest of my family for feeding my book addiction and listening to my stories, and for telling me their stories.

My parents and parents-in-law for their constant love and encouragement, with a special nod to my father, who introduced me to Bilbo and Frodo Baggins many years ago. The road really does go on and on...

Dear Reader,

If you enjoyed reading *Dragon's Truth*, I would appreciate it if you would help others enjoy this book, too. Here are some of the ways you can help spread the word:

Lend it. This book is lending enabled so please share it with a friend.

Recommend it. Help other readers find this book by recommending it to friends, readers' groups, book clubs, and discussion forums.

Share it. Let other readers know you've read the book by positing a note to your social media account and/or your Goodreads account.

Review it. Please tell others why you liked this book by reviewing it on your favorite ebook site.

Everything you do to help others learn about my book is greatly appreciated!

Leanne Pankuch

Plan Your Next Escape!

What's Your Reading Pleasure?

Whether it's captivating historical romance, intriguing mysteries, young adult romance, illustrated children's books, or uplifting love stories, Vinspire Publishing has the adventure for you!

For a complete listing of books available, visit our website at www.vinspirepublishing.com.

Like us on Facebook at
www.facebook.com/VinspirePublishing

Follow us on Twitter at
www.twitter.com/vinspire2004

and follow our blog for details of our upcoming releases, giveaways, author insights, and more!

www.vinspirepublishingblog.com

We are your travel guide to your next adventure

CPSIA information can be obtained
at www.ICGtesting.com
Printed in the USA
LVHW051735070519
616953LV00003B/616/P